A DANGEROUS PASSION: DAN'S STORY

Who *was* Jenny Winslow . . . and why had investigative reporter Dan McGee fallen so hard for this beautiful stranger in top secret trouble? Logic told him that love didn't come from a few days of dodging bullets and a few nights of explosive passion, but for the first time in his footloose life he'd found a woman he could settle down with . . . if her sinister pursuers didn't kill her first. And even if they both got out of this mysterious mess alive, would Dan's modern-day Mata Hari ever hang up her cloak and dagger for good . . . for him. . . ?

A
DANGEROUS
PASSION

by

JoAnn Robb

A SIGNET BOOK

NEW AMERICAN LIBRARY

PUBLISHER'S NOTE

This novel is a work of fiction. Names, characters, places, and incidents either are the product of the author's imagination or are used fictitiously, and any resemblance to actual persons, living or dead, events, or locales is entirely coincidental.

NAL BOOKS ARE AVAILABLE AT QUANTITY DISCOUNTS
WHEN USED TO PROMOTE PRODUCTS OR SERVICES.
FOR INFORMATION PLEASE WRITE TO PREMIUM MARKETING DIVISION.
NEW AMERICAN LIBRARY, 1633 BROADWAY,
NEW YORK, NEW YORK 10019.

Copyright © 1985 by JoAnn Ross

SIGNET, SIGNET CLASSIC, MENTOR, PLUME, MERIDIAN AND NAL BOOKS
are published by New American Library,
1633 Broadway, New York, New York 10019

First Printing, August, 1985

1 2 3 4 5 6 7 8 9

PRINTED IN THE UNITED STATES OF AMERICA

*To my son, Patrick,
at a special time in his life*

Chapter One

"*Don't move, darling, or I'll be forced to pull the trigger.*"

Max Harte had never possessed a talent for prophecy, but as he woke to look down the barrel of a gun, it occurred to him that this was not going to be his day. The twelve-gauge shotgun was intimidating and he didn't move a muscle. It wasn't that Max was afraid to die—he just didn't want to be there when it happened.

"You and me both, Max, old boy," Dan McGee muttered, turning the page of the paperback murder mystery.

"Excuse me?" the woman seated next to him in the crowded airport terminal asked.

"Huh?"

As Dan turned his head, he wondered how he could have missed her arrival. The last guy who sat there wore a leather jacket emblazoned with a skull and crossbones and a gold ring in his left earlobe. This was a definite improvement.

She shook her blond head, obviously confused. There was also something else about her, but she was wearing dark glasses and it was impossible to read the message in her eyes.

"I thought you said something," she explained.

Dan realized he'd been talking to himself again. Which, when he considered the fact that he could have been talking to this lovely lady, was a real waste.

"I must've been reading out loud." He held up the paper-back book in explanation. "I have this habit of losing myself in a story."

As Dan's judicious blue gaze moved from the top of her dark, honey-blond hair, to the curves that were only slightly hidden by her expensive, well-tailored suit, and down her long legs, he wished he'd been reading something different. A heavy tome by Kissinger, perhaps, John Updike's latest novel. Something with class; this woman had it written all over her.

"Oh," she said simply. Her eyes flicked over the garish cover, taking in the female body wearing nothing but a dia-mond the size of a fist.

"I bought this at the gift shop. It's an interesting study of greed and betrayal, actually." He suddenly felt the inexpli-cable need to defend his choice of reading matter. "Have you read any Max Harte novels?"

Her eyes, hidden behind the dark lenses, darted around the terminal like frightened birds. "No."

Despite her definite lack of interest in the conversation, Dan decided to try again. He smiled his boyishly attractive grin that usually worked wonders.

"That's okay. Women probably have different fantasies than men. Are you one of those closet romance readers?"

Not only did the smile not work, he realized, but he'd struck out completely. She suddenly rose from the chair and took off across the flight terminal toward the women's room.

"I wonder if she's sick," he puzzled aloud. "She *was* a lit-tle pale."

He debated whether or not to follow her and wait outside the door, or perhaps even send in the female clerk who was busily checking in passengers, to make sure she was all right.

"Hell, McGee," he muttered, raking his fingers through his black hair, "you're a chump when it comes to women, just like Max Harte. She's a snooty broad, that's all there is to it."

His last words brought a gasp of indignation from the elderly woman who had claimed the empty chair next to him. Her hair was tinted an extraordinary shade of lavender and she was wearing a T-shirt that read *Ladies Sewing Circle and Terrorist Society*. Only in San Francisco, Dan thought. Then he shrugged, tired of explaining his behavior, and returned to his book.

This was the last time, Max Harte vowed. The last time he got mixed up with a gorgeous female whose larcenous instincts outweighed her sex appeal.

"I suppose you want the Princess Carlotta diamond."

Trish smiled. "I've always said you were smarter than you looked, Max. Don't try any stupid heroics. Just give me the diamond and I'll be on my way."

He decided to bluff, buying time. "What if I don't have it?"

She lowered the shotgun to the rumpled sheet, her smile unwavering as she pressed it to the most vulnerable part of his male anatomy. "The diamond, Max. Now."

"Darling, didn't you hear them announce our plane?" The paperback novel was suddenly snatched from his hands. The blonde was back, treating him to a frustrated, but not unpleasant smile. "I swear, leave you alone for ten minutes and you get so deep into those horrible Max Harte books you don't know anything that's going on around you!"

That much was true enough. Dan sure didn't understand this. The elderly woman seated next to him didn't help matters.

"My late husband was the same way," she advised Dan's blond stranger. "I never could keep his nose out of those paperback books. But in his case it was westerns." She imbued the term with an extra helping of scorn as she looked at the novel the blonde was putting into her shoulder bag.

"I suppose all men have their little fantasies," the blonde said, sharing a smile of female superiority with the old woman. "It probably helps them get through the dull routine at the office . . . Oh, I called your mother, darling."

"My mother?" Dan rose, deciding to put an end to this entire farce, but she reached up to press her fingertips against his lips.

"I know. You told me not to worry about Tracy and Travis, and I realize your mother is going to take good care of them while we're away. But after all, sweetheart, it *is* the first time we've both been away from the twins at the same time."

"Twins?"

The old woman shook her head. "Minds like mush. All of them. It makes you wonder how the world's survived this long with men running the show." The look she gave Dan was overtly accusing.

Before Dan could protest, the blonde had looped her arm through his and was practically dragging him to the gate.

"Come along, dear. It really won't do for us to miss our plane. We've been waiting so long for this second honeymoon."

"Honeymoon?" he asked in a low voice as they joined the line of passengers boarding the plane. "You've just piqued my interest, sweetheart."

Her eyes were never still; they circled the waiting area, lighting on each person as if looking for someone in particular. From the tense, white lines around her lips, Dan guessed it was not anyone she was eager to see.

"Please," she murmured, her fingers tightening slightly

on his arm. "Just play along with this and don't ask any questions for the next few minutes."

A warning flashed through his mind, but Dan ignored it. She was lovely, and passing the boring commuter flight to Sacramento with her beat the hell out of Max Harte. He didn't know what she was up to, but far be it from him to turn down anything she had in mind.

He wondered if she was one of those staid executive types who had wild, sexual flings with strangers on out-of-town trips. Despite the thousands of miles he'd traveled, Dan had never met one of these alleged wild women, but he'd read the blurb about them on the cover of *Cosmopolitan* in the gift shop. A guy can always hope, right?

Seats were not assigned on the commuter flight and Dan followed his companion as she made her way to the very back of the plane. The only people he knew who chose these seats were faint-hearted souls who prescribed to the theory that planes always crashed nose first. He thought of asking her if she was afraid of flying, but once again she seemed to have forgotten he existed. Her attention was glued to the door at the front of the airliner, her intent gaze taking in every boarding passenger.

"Would you like me to put that overhead for you?" he asked, noting that she still held the slim attaché case on her lap.

Her fingers tightened on the gray leather. "No, thank you," she said, still watching the other passengers.

It suddenly crossed Dan's mind that she might be watching for her husband. That's all he needed, to be caught helping a runaway wife. Dan reminded himself that, except for her little performance at the gate, she had not been the slightest bit friendly to him. He owed her nothing. If an irate spouse did show up, it was her problem.

"You should probably put it under the seat," he suggested. "It's not a very long flight, but you won't want to hold it on your lap the entire time."

"It's fine."

He shrugged. "Hey, it's your business. I was just trying to help."

The flight crew had closed the door and the woman seemed to relax slightly as she turned toward him. "Thank you. But I'd prefer to hang on to it."

"Whatever you've got in there must be important."

The color drained from her face and Dan couldn't miss the way her fingers tightened on the case once again.

"Who are you?" she whispered.

He reached into the pocket of his rumpled trench coat for a business card, extricating instead a black nylon stocking. He felt the color rise above his collar.

"Wrong pocket."

She almost smiled. "I assumed as much."

The second time he was more successful, pulling out a bent piece of pasteboard. He straightened the corner before handing it to her.

She read the card slowly, and when she lifted her gaze to his, her expression was still wary, but more relaxed. "You're a reporter for *Newsview* magazine?" It was the faintest of whispers.

He nodded.

"What are you doing here? On this flight?"

Dan couldn't tell her the truth, that he was investigating a senator who was rumored to be accepting kickbacks for the construction of government buildings and power plants, so he lied.

"I'm taking a vacation."

She arched a delicate blond brow above her tortoiseshell frames. "Nobody leaves San Francisco to take a vacation in Sacramento."

"I do."

Her eyes narrowed behind the dark lenses and Dan knew she was trying to decide whether or not to trust him with whatever secret of her own she was hiding.

"Can we talk?"

"I thought that's what we'd finally begun to do."

She shook her head. "Not here. When we land. Somewhere more private."

"Sure. Where?" His reporter's nose smelled a story.

He thought she was being a little paranoid as she silently drew a map on the back of his business card, but he'd learned long ago to let his sources tell their stories their own way. Besides, the short hairs were standing up on the back of his neck; the last time that had happened he'd stumbled onto a Pulitzer prize story.

Taking in her full lips and her delicate heart-shaped face, he decided that, even if it turned out to be nothing, having a drink with this woman certainly wouldn't be too hard to take.

He put the card in his wallet when she handed it back to him, then reached into the breast pocket of his coat for his pack of cigarettes. To his amazement, she actually laughed as he pulled out a forgotten bag of soggy French fries.

"Dinner," he explained weakly. "I stopped on the way to the airport and I couldn't carry my luggage and the food all at the same time, so . . ."

His voice dropped off as she took off her glasses momentarily, fixing him with a pair of the largest, softest brown eyes he'd ever seen.

"I'm probably making a big mistake, putting my life in your hands, Dan McGee, but right now you're all I've got."

Life? Goosebumps joined the prickly hairs and Dan knew they were talking about one hell of a story. He might look like one of the most disorganized men who ever crawled out of bed in the morning, but his reporter's instincts were as well honed as a Toledo blade. Putting the French fries aside, he dug a little deeper, still searching for the elusive cigarettes, but when his hand touched the stocking again, he gave up the search.

"You haven't told me your name," he reminded her, trying out his boyish grin again.

She stuck the dark glasses back onto her face and handed him his mystery novel. "Read your book, McGee," she advised. "I'll tell you everything you need to know later." With that, she turned to look out at the night sky.

Dan expelled a harsh sigh as he opened to the dog-eared page. Max Harte had just decided that women were the most frustrating creatures ever put on the earth.

"Amen, brother," Dan muttered, "amen."

He couldn't concentrate on Max's dilemma; his imagination was too busy creating stories about his seatmate. Was she the mistress of a powerful government official carrying proof of the man's high treason? Perhaps she was a defecting Russian ballerina. No. She was too tall—Dan guessed her height to be around five foot eight. And although the suede suit was severely tailored, it was easy to see her feminine curves were fuller than those found on an average ballerina. She could always be a defecting cellist. He'd read about one just last week who'd come to San Francisco on a world tour and suddenly locked herself in the bathroom of the San Francisco opera house, requesting political asylum.

"Do you play the cello?" he asked suddenly.

She turned from the window, eyeing him curiously. "No. Why?"

He shrugged. "Just a crazy thought I had."

"I don't imagine it was the first." Her slight smile softened the words and Dan decided not to take offense.

"And it probably won't be the last, " he agreed. "Do you play any instrument?"

"Sorry."

"That's okay. Like I said, it was a crazy idea anyway. You wouldn't happen to speak Russian would you?"

Her eyes widened. "Of course not." Her gaze held new interest. "Do you?"

"No."

"Then why—?"

"Promise not to laugh?"

She nodded. "Promise."

"I hoped you might be a Russian defector."

"I'm sorry."

Dan shrugged and reached into his pocket again, finally locating the pack of cigarettes. "That's okay. I'd probably just end up getting shot trying to protect you, anyway."

He held the pack out to her and couldn't miss the fact that her hands trembled as she extracted a cigarette. She was still far more nervous than this casual conversation indicated.

The arrival of the flight attendant forestalled any further discussion. Dan knew it was chauvinistic, but he preferred the old days when flight attendants were called stewardesses and were young, attractive females who dressed in miniskirts. This one was a young, attractive male who was wearing a pair of tight pants that Dan supposed women passengers found every bit as enticing as those short skirts he remembered so fondly.

"Would you like something to drink?"

"I'll have a beer," Dan replied. "Whatever you have, I'm not choosy." He turned to the woman next to him, deciding that for whatever reason, she's probably want to keep up this marriage charade for the duration of the flight. "What would you like, dear?"

It proved to be an extremely difficult decision. "Nothing, thank you . . . No, I think I'll have a cup of coffee. Black, no sugar." As the attendant began to pour the drink she changed her mind once again. "On second thought, I can probably do without the caffeine."

From the way her hand was shaking as she drew in on that cigarette, Dan concurred wholeheartedly. She eyed the bottles on the chrome cart, as if the choice was suddenly very important.

"I think I'd like a Bloody Mary, please."

Dan noted absently that the attendant dumped the paper cup of coffee into a plastic trash bag. That seemed a waste. If it had been him, Dan would have saved it for the next passenger who ordered coffee. No wonder the airlines were losing money.

Dan pulled the tray down in front of him. She still hadn't released her hold on the attaché case, making it impossible to lower hers.

"We'll share," he said, taking her drink from the young man and placing it beside his plastic glass of lukewarm beer.

"Thank you. For everything," she said suddenly.

As her gaze locked with his, Dan knew they were talking about a lot more than sharing a table.

She stumbled slightly as they made their way down the ramp to the terminal and Dan reached out, catching her arm to steady her.

"Are you all right?"

"I'm fine," she said in a shaky voice that didn't instill a great deal of confidence.

"You're flushed. I think you've got a fever." He stopped, putting the back of his hand against her forehead. Her skin seemed a little warm, but he couldn't be certain.

She jerked away. "You're calling attention to us," she

hissed, beginning to move down the expanse of orange carpeting.

"Well, excuse me. I just thought it might also catch the notice of whomever it is you're hiding from if you collapsed in the middle of the Sacramento Airport."

"Touché," she murmured. "I'm sorry. It's just that all this is so new to me."

"All what?"

She shook her head. "Not here. Later, when we meet."

He put his hand on her waist, and she gave him a startled glance as she tried to pull away. "Hey," he said under his breath, "it's okay. I'm allowed to put my arm around you; after all, I've seen you naked . . . . Besides, you're not all that steady on your feet, sweetheart."

She stopped in her tracks. "When have you seen me naked?"

He waggled his dark brows in what he'd always thought was a fair-to-middling John Belushi imitation. "Now the woman wants to talk dirty in public. I'm your husband, remember? Unless Tracy and Travis arrived UPS, we've done some playing around."

She shook her head. "I think you're crazy, McGee."

He leaned down, planting a quick, unexpected kiss on her lips. The impulsive action surprised Dan as much as it did her. "Probably. It's the only thing that would explain playing along with this game of yours."

"That and the chance for another Pulitzer," she murmured, pressing her fingertips experimentally against her lips.

"You know about that?"

"Your Koreagate stories were brilliant. You deserved that award."

Dan felt his chest expanding and didn't remember ever

experiencing such a rush of pride. Not even when receiving the notification. "You've read my stuff?"

Her lips twitched slightly. "Fishing for compliments?"

"Hell, no," he said quickly; a little too quickly. Dan laughed. "All right. Maybe just a little."

He'd expected a smile, but as she stopped slowly and looked up at him, her expression was unnervingly sober. "You've got a reputation for being a real straight shooter, Daniel Patrick McGee. That's the reason I'm going to give you a story that reaches all the way to Washington."

"D.C.?"

"Not the state," she agreed.

"Gee, and here I thought it was my boyish charm and sex appeal that earned me an invitation to share a drink with a sexy stranger in some out of the way, romantic inn."

Her eyes were still shielded by the glasses, but he could see the slight amusement in them as they took a slow, judicious tour of his body. He tried to stand up a little straighter and sucked in his gut. Too many fast-food meals, he rued, vowing to take up jogging first thing tomorrow morning.

"Don't push your luck. It's still coming as a shock that Dan McGee, White Knight, comes in such a disheveled package."

Dan decided that, as soon as he checked into the hotel, he was sending his coat out to be cleaned. And his suit, since it hadn't been pressed for the last three cities. The next time she saw him, he'd look like something right out of *Gentlemen's Quarterly*. Dan sighed, knowing that to be an impossible dream.

"Want to rent a car?" he asked as they entered the main terminal.

"I've got one waiting," she answered. "I'll leave first; then you wait twenty minutes and follow me. I don't want anyone to see us together."

"I thought we were suppose to be married."

Her eyes had begun their nervous darting again and she shrugged away from his touch. "That was in San Francisco. We're in Sacramento now."

"Wow, talk about quickie divorces. What about the kids?"

"Kids?" she asked absently, her gaze sweeping the room once more.

"Tracy and Travis. My mother's a softhearted old soul, but she's not going to look kindly on us dumping the twins on her permanently."

She didn't return his smile. "I've got to go," she said abruptly. "I'll see you in about a half hour at the inn on the map."

She was gone before he could say another word. As he watched her walk toward the automatic glass doors, Dan noticed that her gait was anything but steady. Damn, she could hardly walk, how in the hell did she think she was going to drive?

He discovered belatedly that Sacramento was a PGA tour city. As he tried to catch up with her, Dan was suddenly surrounded by a crowd of admirers, all carrying placards welcoming one golfer or another.

"Are you Jimmy Harrison?" one winsome redhead inquired, standing directly in front of him.

Dan shifted to the left, trying to get around her. "No, I'm not."

She was quicker, blocking his forward progress. "You look like him."

"Believe me, I'm not." He tried a lateral move to the right.

She wasn't giving up easily. "Are you sure?"

Dan decided he'd been polite long enough. He lifted the woman off her feet and moved her to the side. "Sorry, lady, but you're in my way." He ignored her sputtered protest as he jogged to the front doors.

She was gone. Dan stared out into the darkness, his heart sinking as he watched a heavy rainfall turn the asphalt streets into a sheet of black glass. As he went back inside, taking a wide path around the golf fans on his way to the rental counter, he realized suddenly that he cared very much what happened to his mysterious stranger—and it had nothing to do with his chances for a big story.

Dan tried to clear his mind and answer the questions the attractive rental agent was asking. Damn, he thought, as he took the keys and raced toward the parking lot, I don't even know her name!

Chapter Two

Leaning forward, Dan tried to see through the rippling film of water streaming down the windshield. He was unfamiliar with the city, and kept consulting her quickly sketched map as he drove along South River Road.

The heavy clouds blocked out any light that might come from the moon or stars, and the view outside was a dark, vast well. He cursed himself for letting her leave alone when he saw the scene of the accident.

A compact car had skidded off the road and was front down in a ditch. The flashing red lights and the swinging yellow beams of the flashlights added an eerie effect to the accident. Pulling abruptly off to the side of the road, Dan parked behind a black-and-white patrol car, instinctively knowing he would find her here.

"Hey, mister, you're not allowed over there!"

A young patrolman put out an arm to block his progress, but Dan wasn't in any mood to worry about the consequences. He pushed his way past the uniformed officer, the rain pelting down on him as he ran toward the car.

"Oh, my God," he groaned, reaching for her as he recognized her blond hair spread out on the front seat. Her pale brow was darkened with blood, a sight that tore at something inside him.

A second patrolman grabbed his arm, jerking him backwards. "Not so fast, buddy," he warned. "We've already called for the paramedics. Nobody moves her until then."

Dan was frantic. "You idiots! She needs help."

The man's face was like carved granite. "You go moving her without knowing what you're doing, buster, and you might make things a lot worse.

Dan reluctantly acknowledged the man had a point. "When's the ambulance getting here?"

"Any time now. Who are you? And what do you know about the lady?"

"I'm Dan McGee."

"What's her name?"

Feeling like a damned fool, Dan hedged. "Come on, officer, surely you've already found her ID."

The man's eyes narrowed as he fixed Dan with a suspicious gaze. "She doesn't have any on her. So it looks like it's up to you to let us know who we've got here."

Dan couldn't believe that. She had carried a suede purse with a shoulder strap. He'd seen it swinging as she left the terminal. And the attaché case. Surely that would have a name tag on it?

"What about her purse? And her attaché case?"

"I already told you, the car's clean. Trunk too." His gray eyes held a dangerous glitter that flashed in the rotating glow of the patrol car light. "Why don't you show me some ID of your own, Mr. McGee?"

Dan shrugged, his mind whirling as he tried to figure out what had happened to her things. There was one possible answer, but that was so outrageous he wasn't prepared to tell this patrolman.

"Sure," he agreed. "It's right here." He reached into his breast pocket.

"Not so fast." The younger officer joined them. "Why don't you put your hands on the top of the car and spread your legs? Real slow." The words, couched as a request, were an unmistakable command.

Dan obliged, looking over at the woman whose name he didn't even know. He didn't like the way she was all alone, unconscious, with the rain drifting into the car.

"Shouldn't someone be with her?"

The older man's gaze moved from Dan to the disabled rental car and back to Dan. "I think we'd better stay here with you right now," he decided. "Until you can give us a little information."

Dan muttered a low, harsh oath as the younger man patted him down.

"No weapons," he stated finally.

"I could have told you that," Dan said through gritted teeth. "Damn it, can't you at least put a blanket over her? She's getting wet!"

"Why don't you just let us do our job our own way?" the older patrolman suggested, nevertheless pulling a plaid blanket out of the trunk of the police car which he draped over her. His expression was grim as he returned to Dan.

"Now, Mr. McGee, I'd appreciate seeing some ID. If you don't mind."

Dan was fuming as he tried to remember where he'd stuck his wallet. He reached into his pocket, pulling out the cigarettes and placing the pack on the roof of the patrol car.

"I've got it here somewhere," he said, beginning to sweat despite the falling rain.

As if he didn't have enough trouble, the next thing he pulled out was the black stocking. The patrolmen exchanged a meaningful glance and the younger one dropped his hand ever so casually to the revolver he wore on his hip.

"Does that happen to belong to the young lady?" the older of the two inquired carefully.

"No, it's mine," he answered recklessly, knowing that was probably only going to get him in deeper.

From the look in the men's eyes, he knew he'd guessed correctly. He dug in his pocket once more, this time pulling out the crumpled business card.

"Here. Here's my card."

The older patrolman read it under the yellow beam of his flashlight. "It's a business card all right," he acknowledged. "But how am I supposed to know if it's yours or not?"

Good point. Dan dug in again, this time feeling a rush of relief as his fingers closed around his ancient, scarred leather wallet.

He studied it for a long, silent time. "Yep, that press pass photo looks like you. You're a reporter, huh?"

"Yeah."

"In town on business?"

"Vacation."

"I see. And the young lady? Who did you say she is?"

"My wife." The answer came off the top of his head and Dan held his breath, waiting for one of the men to realize the obvious flaw.

"I see . . . I've got a little problem with that, Mr. McGee. You see, we ran a check on her license plate. That's a rental car." He took off his hat, seemingly oblivious to the rain as he scratched his head in a gesture Dan knew was feigned. He was drawing this questioning out to make Dan sweat and it was working too damn well.

"It is."

"Uh-huh. But this slip in your wallet indicates you're driving a rental car, too."

Dan's heart sank. "That's right."

The man rubbed his chin. "Isn't it a little odd for a man and wife to rent separate cars if they're driving along the same road?"

. Dan's imagination kicked into overdrive. "We got into a little spat in the airport over my mother. She's taking care of the kids, and uh, Mary, can't believe they'll be okay for two weeks. She wanted to give up the idea of a second honeymoon."

The two officers nodded as they considered his words. Dan figured they were remembering spats they'd had with their own wives. He said a silent prayer and continued with the quickly fabricated lie.

"I went into the bar to have a drink, and when I came out, she'd already rented a car and left. The only place I could think she'd go was the inn where we booked a room, so I rented a second car and took off after her."

The crack in his voice was not feigned. "I never expected to find this."

At that moment, the ambulance arrived with a wail of its siren. "So her name is Mary McGee?"

"That's it," Dan proved himself an adroit liar, figuring she'd receive medical care a lot faster if he gave her an identity. She'd already proclaimed them married; it wasn't his fault she'd never told him her name.

The patrolman appeared to accept his explanation. "Don't worry, Mr. McGee," he assured Dan. "I've seen a lot worse. Your wife is going to be fine."

"I hope so," Dan replied fervently, watching as the paramedics carefully extracted the unconscious woman from the wrecked car. "She has to be."

He was allowed to ride with her in the back of the ambulance, while the younger patrolman followed in his rental car. Dan regretted his lie as the attendants continually tried to rouse the unconscious woman by calling her name. She did not respond to Mary and he wished he'd been able to give them her real name. Anything to reach her. Her lashes were a dark fringe against cheeks so horribly pale they looked like newly driven snow.

"Her pulse is pretty weak," the paramedic stated, lifting her lids. Dan cringed when he saw how glazed her lovely brown eyes were. "Any chance she's taken anything? Her pupils are awfully dilated."

"This lady would never do drugs," Dan snapped. He knew it was the truth without knowing why.

"Sure looks like something to me," the man mused aloud.

Dan suddenly remembered the flight attendant throwing out the coffee after she'd changed her drink order. It was shortly after that that she seemed flushed and unsteady. Damn, what kind of protection was he? In the last two hours she'd been drugged and had run her car off the road in what could have been a fatal accident. He groaned.

"Remember something?" The paramedic didn't look surprised. Dan decided drug-related accidents were probably run of the mill in his business.

"She had a drink on the plane," he stated slowly. "After that, she seemed to be a little dizzy and flushed."

"One drink?"

The young man unbuttoned an extra button on her silk blouse, putting his stethoscope against her chest. Dan was surprised by her lacy underwear. He'd expected something more tailored. Obviously this woman was full of surprises. He only hoped he could keep her alive long enough to discover some of the more interesting ones.

"Only one. A Bloody Mary."

"This doesn't look like the result of one drink."

Dan reached out and took her hand in his, needing some physical contact. It was so damned cold. "I know," he muttered, "but I think she got more than she ordered."

"We'll have the blood work done as soon as we get her

into emergency. The sooner we know what's she's ingested, the sooner we can get to work on her."

"Just hurry," he instructed the man. "For God's sake, hurry."

"You look awful."

At the sound of her soft voice, Dan woke with a start. Every muscle in his body protested having spent the night crammed into the hard plastic chair.

"You're awake."

"I think so. Or else this is one dreary dream. Are the walls of this room really painted muddy green?"

"That's right," he said with the enthusiasm one might give to a winner of the sixty-four thousand dollar question.

"And is this tube really stuck into my arm?"

"The IV," he agreed. "It's a saline solution to wash out any remaining drugs."

"I don't take drugs," she answered automatically.

Dan shook his head. "The Bloody Mary on the plane was spiked with more than vodka. You were damned lucky, you know; someone was trying to kill you."

She grimaced, lifting her fingers to her forehead, which was swathed in a thick bandage. "Yeah, real lucky. What do I look like? And what plane?"

He was so pleased to see a spark of vanity, he missed her second question. "You're beautiful."

She shook her head, then from the pain that flashed in her brown eyes looked as if she wished she hadn't. "You really are a terrible liar, Dan McGee. Do I look as bad as you?"

He ran his palm over his stubbled beard and combed his unruly black curls with his fingertips, knowing it wouldn't do any good.

"Impossible. Nobody can look as bad as I do in the morning."

She reached out a hand, covering his. "I take that back. I can't imagine anyone looking quite so good to me as you do." Her gaze was soft as it moved over his face with the impact of a tender caress. "Although you do look dead on your feet. How long have you been here?"

"A few hours."

"What time is it?"

"Morning. About seven."

"Have you been here with me all night?"

He shrugged, trying for a casual response. "Hey, I didn't know anyone else in town."

"You don't know me," she reminded him.

His eyes held hers and Dan wondered what kind of man had lustful thoughts about a woman in her weak condition.

"I have every intention of taking care of that little matter as soon as we get you out of here."

She looked deep into his eyes, searching. Before she could respond, the door flew open and they were joined by a nurse who had obviously just come on duty. She was not from the legion who had tried to establish official visiting hours last night. Not that they'd gotten away with it, of course. Dan had taken possession of the chair next to her bed the minute she was brought up from the emergency room and it would have taken a lot more than a few officious females to blast him out of it.

"Well, what have we here? A visitor? At this hour of the morning?"

Dan simply glared in response, slouching lower into the chair.

She shook a ruddy finger at him. "Don't get your back up, Mr. McGee, I've already been warned about you. You were the talk of the ward last night. Livened things up considerably, you did. And how are we this morning, Mary?" The nurse stuck a thermometer in her mouth and picked up her wrist, counting off the pulse beats on her watch.

Confused brown eyes asked for an explanation. "I know you didn't have any ID with you, dear," Dan said quickly. "But I told the officers your name. Mary McGee."

She seemed not to mind the new name, but he hastened to explain before she blew his cover. "Next time you take off in a huff, you should remember to take something in the car with you. It's just lucky I came along when I did."

He felt like a hypocrite. If he'd come along ten minutes sooner, he could have protected her. If he'd stopped to think about that flight attendant, he could have prevented her from taking the damn drug in the first place. His blood turned to ice as he realized she was supposed to be dead this morning.

"Lucky," she murmured, not appearing to blame him for anything.

"Let's keep our mouth closed, dear, or we won't get a proper reading," the nurse advised.

The woman managed a slight smile that she shared with Dan. He tried to give one back, but felt too guilty. They remained silent as the nurse finished up her morning duties and promised that breakfast would be delivered within the hour.

"Breakfast," she groaned. "I couldn't eat a thing. Why is my throat so sore?"

"They had to pump your stomach."

"Oh. Of course. I hadn't thought of that . . . Thanks for the use of your name."

"Anytime. Although I think since we've been married for two days now, it's about time I learned my bride's name. Not to mention the mother of those darling twins, Tracy and Travis."

"Tracy and Travis?" She sounded honestly confused.

"The kids. You remember."

She furrowed her brow. "No."

Dan was growing a little worried. "You made them up," he prompted, "in the airport."

"Airport?"

He didn't like the way this conversation was going. "The San Francisco airport. Remember? You came up with some line about us being married and leaving the twins with my mother while we had a second honeymoon in Sacramento."

"In Sacramento? We left San Francisco to have a honeymoon in Sacramento?" Her tone was incredulous.

He laced their fingers together, trying not to squeeze too tightly in his distress. "Hey," he said, hoping against hope that she was joking, "I just figured you had more beauty than brains."

"Are we in Sacramento now?"

"I'm getting the doctor," he decided.

"Wait. Why are we in Sacramento?"

Now he *was* scared. "I don't know. You were bringing some papers to someone. All you'd tell me is that it was a big story and reached all the way to Washington."

"D.C.?"

"Not the state," he muttered.

"And that's why someone was trying to kill me?"

He nodded, the lump in his throat not permitting words.

"I think we're in trouble," she whispered, turning whiter than the starched pillowcase. "Because I can't remember anything."

"That's ridiculous," he blurted out. "You remember me. And you didn't even meet me until last night."

She looked genuinely puzzled. "That is odd, isn't it?"

"What's odd?" Dan was torn between relief and regret as the doctor who'd admitted her last night strolled into the room. He picked up the clipboard from the end of the bed, scanning the illegible notes.

"Well, Mrs. McGee, you're looking a lot more chipper than you did last time I saw you. How do you feel?"

"Fine. But I'm having trouble with my memory, doctor."

He nodded. "That's to be expected. That's quite a lump on your head. You're bound to suffer from temporary amnesia about the events immediately preceding the accident."

"She remembers some spotty things," Dan offered.

The young doctor nodded. "That's a little unusual, of course. But there's nothing to worry about."

Dan only wished that were true. She obviously shared his concern.

"When will my memory return?"

The physician shrugged, giving her a broad, professional smile. "Most everything that happened should come back a little at a time. The trick is not to force it."

"Most everything?"

He flashed the penlight into her eyes. "Most everything," he confirmed. "Of course, there may be permanent gaps. It's impossible to tell exactly what damage you've done, hitting your head on the steering wheel like that. And the drugs.

"By the way, the authorities are looking into it, but at the moment it appears you were the victim of another lunatic who put the drugs into random cans of Bloody Mary mix at the factory. There's an order out for that batch to be recalled before we suffer any more unfortunate incidents."

Dan knew the attack was anything but random, but at this time he didn't want to confuse the issue. Especially since he didn't know anything about it. And what was more frightening, she didn't either.

"It wasn't a random accident, was it?" she asked once they were alone again.

He shook his head.

"I can't remember why. But I do recall that I was frightened. And of all the people in the airport, you looked like a man I could trust."

He would have preferred to think of himself as one of those dangerous types, the kind women swooned over in novels. But, in this case, he decided safe was rather nice, too.

"I'm glad you chose me," he said honestly.

"Me too. Oh, and McGee?"

He arched a black brow. "Yeah?"

"My name is Jennifer. Jennifer Winslow."

"Jenny," he tried it out. "I like that; it suits you."

"Do you know, I've never let anyone call me Jenny before. But from you I think I like it, too." She smiled, then wearily leaned her head back against the pillow.

He brushed her blond bangs off her forehead with a gentle touch. "Get some rest, Jenny Winslow. You've earned it."

She nodded sleepily, drifting off as he gave her a long, thoughtful look.

Chapter Three

Dan's anxious gaze swept over Jennifer as he entered the hospital room, his arms filled with boxes. Her smile was steadier, there was more color in her cheeks, and the way her eyes lit up upon seeing him did funny things to his heart.

"You're looking better."

"Thanks. I'm feeling a lot better, actually. In fact, the nurse was just in to tell me I was going to get sprung." Her gaze narrowed, taking in the packages. "What's all this?"

"Clothes."

She nodded approvingly. "Good idea. You could use a new suit."

He glanced down, realizing that spending the night in the wet gray suit had permanently ironed in several new wrinkles. He wondered why he hadn't noticed that when he'd showered and changed shirts at the hotel.

"This one still has a few more miles in it," he defended his well-traveled clothing.

Her brown eyes twinkled with laughter, and Dan realized it was the first time he'd seen her relaxed. "I suppose, if you're thinking about becoming a hobo. Besides, I haven't seen lapels that wide since—oh, 1976."

"Seventy four," he corrected. "And the wide lapels suit me. I'm a big man; it's all a matter of proportion."

She laughed. "You'd have to wear the same size as Big Foot to be proportional to those lapels. If you didn't buy a new suit, what's in the boxes?"

"Clothes for you." He felt a little apprehensive about what had seemed a perfect idea a few hours before. "Your suit was wet and stained and since you didn't have any luggage, I picked up some things for you to wear out of here."

Her gaze was both tender and wary at the same time. "That's incredibly sweet, McGee. Did you say you'd picked them out?"

He squared his shoulders a little in self-defense. "Hey, why don't you just withhold judgment until you see them, okay?"

Her smile was conciliatory. "Okay."

Dan piled the boxes on the bed and lit a cigarette as he waited nervously for her to take the ribbon off the first package. It had probably been silly to have them gift wrapped, he decided, wondering what had spurred the romantic impulse.

"This is beautiful paper," she murmured, using her fingernails to carefully cut the tape. "I'm going to save it."

It figured, Dan thought, drawing in on the cigarette. In the rare instance he was given a gift, he'd tear into it, not caring about the wrapping. He decided there were two kinds of people in the world; neat ones and sloppy ones. And opening presents was probably one of the best test methods to sort them out.

"Oh, Dan," Jenny exclaimed, holding up a light-rose lace teddy that heightened the returning color in her cheeks, "it's lovely!" She smiled, a dancing light in her eyes. "And the right size, too. You must have a great deal of experience buying women's lingerie."

He knew she was remembering that damned nylon. Where was amnesia when you needed it? Oh well, he thought, that's what he got for trying to be neat. For the first time in his life, he'd looked under a hotel bed before checking out. That particular item of feminine apparel had somehow been left behind after a pleasant interlude with a UPI reporter in New York. He'd unconsciously stuffed it in his pocket and completely forgotten about it until that incident on the plane.

"Not really. I just kept going to department stores until I found a lingerie clerk who looked about your size."

"That's very clever."

"I thought so."

"Did you have her model it, too?" Jenny teased lightly.

Dan's gaze turned warm as it moved over her. "No," he answered slowly. "I hoped you'd give me that particular honor." He was teasing, but not completely.

She dropped her eyes to the remaining packages. "I can't wait to see what else you bought," she said on a false, cheery note.

Dan hid a slight sigh and lowered his body into a chair. A significant little silence filled the room as she seemed to be taking an extraordinarily long time with the wrapping paper. He exhaled a cloud of blue smoke, watching with apparent fascination as it rose to the acoustical tiled ceiling.

"Daniel McGee! You shouldn't have done this."

Dan felt a spasm of apprehension. "You don't like it," he said flatly.

Her eyes were wide with pleasure as she stroked the knit dress. "It's the most beautiful, romantic dress I've ever seen."

The icy fist that had been twisting in his stomach loosened its grip. "You really like it?"

Her face was hidden by a veil of honey-blond hair as she gazed down at the pink dress on her lap. "Is this how you see me?" she asked in a barely audible voice.

Dan knew it might be a trick question, but decided to

answer it honestly. At this point, he didn't have anything to lose. "Yes. I hope I haven't offended you."

Jenny laughed softly. "No. Not at all." She lifted her head and her brown eyes engaged Dan's with honest interest. "I'm just surprised you managed to discover my secret so quickly. I can't remember another man ever being so intuitive."

"Your secret?" He had the feeling her crooked little smile was directed inward.

"I'm a closet romantic," she admitted softly. There was a slight challenge in her gaze now, as if daring him to laugh.

Dan had no such intention. "Bingo," he breathed with a heartfelt sigh of relief. Things were definitely looking up.

"Bingo?" She arched a blond brow, inviting elaboration.

He shrugged, suddenly feeling self-conscious about this conversation. "While you were sleeping, I counted all the things we don't have in common. It looked pretty hopeless for a while."

"And now?"

He thought he saw an invitation gleaming in her brown eyes, but cautioned himself not to jump to conclusions. "I think two unabashed romantics just might manage to find some common ground, don't you?"

"I knew you were a throwback, Dan McGee," she alleged. "Even before I knew who you were, I told myself that if I needed a white knight, that giant teddy bear reading the dirty book was it."

"That wasn't a dirty book," he defended automatically. Then he frowned. "Wait a minute—teddy bear?"

Her smile was not cruel. "I can't help it if you remind me of a huge, huggable teddy bear, McGee."

Whatever happened to tigers and panthers? he wondered miserably. Women were always comparing Max Harte to some lean jungle animal. A teddy bear?

"That's a compliment," she murmured softly, as if reading his mind.

Dan grunted in response, deciding she'd probably done irreparable damage to his ego.

"Hey," she said, "come over here and let me thank you properly."

Jenny held out her arms and there was some force in her that was irresistible. Dan slowly stubbed out his cigarette as she moved the clothing and empty boxes aside, patting the sheet beside her. The mattress sagged as he sat on the edge of the bed.

"I don't want to hurt you."

"You won't."

"You've been through a lot, Jenny. You're bound to be pretty vulnerable right now."

Her gaze captured his with a strength that belied her weakened physical condition. "I'm a grown woman, Dan. I know what I want. And right now I want you to kiss me."

Oh, God, that was what he wanted too. He realized suddenly that that was what he'd wanted since he'd looked up from Max Harte's latest adventure to see the seat next to him occupied by an angel. He shifted, bracing himself with his arms as he slowly lowered his head to her inviting lips.

Dan could have wrung the neck of the overly cheery floor nurse as she chose exactly that moment to come sweeping into the room in a swirl of starched white skirt.

"Well, well, are we all ready to go?" She wagged her finger at Dan, who decided that if she did it one more time, he'd bite it off. "Really, Mr. McGee, you must have some restraint. Your poor wife has been through quite an ordeal in the last twenty-four hours."

As his body throbbed with unrequited need, Dan wanted to say that all this hadn't exactly been a picnic for him, either, but he remained silent. Jenny reached up, stroking his cheek, soothing the muscle jerking along his jawline with her fingertips.

"I'll get dressed so we can leave," she murmured.

Dan caught her hand, pressing a kiss into the soft skin of her palm, his blue eyes locked to hers as they exchanged a private message.

Then he released her, giving her a light, unthreatening pat on the hip. "Hurry up, sweetheart," he instructed in his best James Cagney impression, "I think it's time we blew this joint."

She grinned, her eyes alight with shared mischief. "High time."

Dan took the time Jenny was dressing to attend to the mountains of paperwork involved in her release. He didn't want to make waves with *Newsview's* insurance department by suddenly adding a heretofore unmentioned wife onto his group policy, and he sure didn't want to call unwelcome attention to them by changing the records to her own name, just in case someone out there was checking hospital admissions for Jennifer Winslow.

"I can take a credit card," the clerk stated dryly, looking at the growing pile of odds and ends on her counter. There were two ticket stubs from a Detroit Tigers game he'd seen last month, a ticket from the hotel dry cleaner who was hopefully improving his trench coat, and two pages of wrinkled expense account forms he kept forgetting to mail in to the office.

Along with all that was a racing form from Santa Anita— all the circled horses had been losers—and an address book that had lost its cover as well as all the "A" and "B" listings somewhere in El Salvador. That had turned out to be a minor inconvenience in the beginning, but eventually he settled into a workable pattern: he hadn't dated any woman whose last name started with the beginning of the alphabet in the last few years.

"I've got my checkbook," he assured her, digging into yet another pocket. "It'll just take another minute."

She snorted, a most unfeminine sound, as Dan pulled out a bright yellow piece of paper. He smoothed it out on the counter, recognizing the telegram his mother had sent him a few months ago, requesting money to post bond somewhere in Greenland. His wide brow furrowed. He *had* remembered to send it, hadn't he? He'd hate to think of Lillian McGee rotting away in some arctic jail, all in the name of baby harp seals.

The clerk cleared her throat noisily and Dan decided that his mother had been taking care of herself long before his birth. She'd be all right. The telegram joined the other artifacts on the pyramid-shaped pile, and his hand delved into the pocket once again.

"Eureka!" He pulled out the checkbook with a flourish.

"At last," the woman muttered, seemingly unimpressed.

Dan patted his breast pocket, wondering where he'd left his pen.

"Here. I assume you want to get your wife home in this decade." The clerk handed him a pen, apparently unwilling to wait for another searching expedition.

Dan grinned his appreciation, noticing with dismay that it wasn't working any better on this officious female than it had yesterday on Jenny. He worried that he might be losing his touch, just when he was going to need every ounce of dubious charm he possessed.

"Thanks," he said flatly, depressed by that thought. He filled in the blanks on the plain brown check in a wide, looping hand and tore it off the register hurriedly, wanting to get out of the situation before his self-confidence was undermined further.

"You tore off the date."

He looked down at the ragged edge of the check and sighed. "Here, I'll just fit it in."

The woman eyed the check with blatant disdain. "Why don't you write me another one?" she suggested. "Since this one seems to have something all over it, anyway."

He plucked the wrinkled piece of paper from her fingers, looking at it with renewed interest. "Oh, that's just coffee stains. The bank will still cash it."

The clerk shut her eyes for a long, silent moment. "Why don't you stick the date on here somewhere, Mr. McGee, so we can both get on with our business?"

He shrugged, wondering why, if she didn't like people, the woman had chosen a job where she had to deal with them all day.

"Sure." He re-dated the check and handed it back to her.

"Finally," she said with a sigh of relief. She turned away, carrying the check gingerly between her fingers as if it were still dripping with wet coffee. "Oh, Mr. McGee?"

"Yeah?"

She peered at him through her bifocals. "Tell your wife I admire her. She must be an incredibly brave woman."

He smiled at that, thinking how much Jenny had been through in the last twenty-four hours. "She sure is that," he agreed cheerily.

It was not until he was in the elevator, on the way to the fifth floor, that Dan realized exactly what the woman had meant by her remark. He vowed that from this moment on, he would not give Jenny any reason to regret that she'd chosen him to be her champion. All it would take to become a paragon of efficiency was a slight mental adjustment. He was an intelligent man; he could pull it off.

"A piece of cake," he said under his breath as the heavy steel doors opened onto Jenny's floor. He jammed his large hands into the back pockets of his slacks and, whistling happily, made his way down the hall to her room.

She was standing by the window, obviously ready and waiting. Even from the back he could tell the dress was a perfect fit.

"Ready to go?"

She turned eagerly in his direction, her smile letting him know exactly how happy she was that he'd returned.

"I was beginning to miss you."

"I was only gone twenty minutes."

Her gaze was solemn. "I know. A very long twenty minutes."

As Dan's heart began to pound in a rhythm that could not possibly be normal, it crossed his mind that if this was a heart attack, he couldn't have it in a better place than a hospital.

"You look beautiful." The statement, which he'd issued so automatically over the years, came out as a ragged croak.

She held her hands out, turning slowly for his approval. "It's the dress," she murmured.

Dan's eyes feasted on her. The pastel-pink knit dress hugged her curves in a way that displayed every feminine attribute. The modestly low cut neckline allowed a view of the slight swelling of her breasts, and Dan felt his body stirring as they rose and fell under his heated appraisal.

"The outfit is only window dressing. It's the lady who's the beauty."

She blushed slightly at the fervor in his tone. "I'll pay you back for everything as soon as I get home to San Francisco," she murmured, her hands smoothing nervously at nonexistent wrinkles on her skirt.

"That's ridiculous," he refused instantly.

"No, it's not. I'm used to paying my own way, McGee." Her back stiffened a little and Dan had to remind himself that, despite her vulnerable appearance, this lady had already proven she had the heart of a lion.

He attempted a different tack. "I'm sure you are," he agreed. "And we'll talk about the hospital bill later. But the clothes are on me, Jenny."

She opened her mouth to object and for the first time Dan welcomed the arrival of the floor nurse. "Oh, don't you look pretty," she gushed. "I'd give anything to be able to wear knits." She gazed down with good-natured humor at her ample frame. "Believe it or not, I used to be a skinny little thing like you. Six kids finally did me in."

"We've got two," Dan volunteered, causing Jenny to shoot him a warning look.

"Isn't that nice? Boys or girls?"

"One of each. Travis and Tracy. They're twins."

"That's smart. If you're going to be pregnant, you might as well double the payoff." The woman grinned. "You sure kept your figure, honey. How old are they?"

At Jennifer's confused expression, Dan jumped in. "My wife is having a little trouble with her memory. They're eight."

The nurse's head bobbed approvingly. "That's a nice age. Able to help around the house, but not old enough to give you any of that teenage trouble." She patted Jennifer's arm. "And don't you worry, as soon as Mr. McGee gets you home to your kids, it'll all come back.

"You know, I see a lot in this business and believe me, honey, there are a lot of guys who can't be bothered with their wives' illnesses. But this one," she jerked her head in Dan's direction, "will stick like glue until you're one hundred percent."

"Like glue," Dan agreed cheerfully, earning a sharp look from Jennifer which he steadfastly ignored. "Speaking of husbandly gestures, Nurse—" he glanced at the name tag pinned to her ample bosom"—Long, don't you think a man has the right to surprise his wife with a new dress once in a while? Even if she's the independent type who likes to buy her own clothes?"

His expression was absolutely innocent, although he could feel Jenny's rising irritation.

"Absolutely." This time the finger was wagged in Jenny's direction. "You're a lucky woman. This one's a keeper." With that she waved her arm, directing Jenny into the wheelchair she'd brought with her.

"I'd rather walk."

"No such luck, hon. Hospital policy. It wouldn't do to have you get dizzy and fall and sue us now, would it?"

Jenny's sigh of frustration ruffled her bangs as she sulkily threw her body into the wheelchair. Dan realized, not for the first time, that he was dealing with a stubborn, albeit intriguing, woman. She was going to take some careful handling, and he knew she wasn't going to accept his plan easily.

In fact, she'd probably blow sky high when she heard it. He wondered if it would be cheating to take her on a prolonged tour of the city to wear her out so she couldn't march out of the hotel and head back to San Francisco on her own. Because, whether she liked it or not, he wasn't letting her out of his sight until they found the person or persons who were so intent on harming her.

"Convenient," she murmured, not blinking an eye as he stood aside to let her enter the hotel room. The trench coat, encased in plastic, lay draped on one of the double beds, giving mute testimony to the fact that this was Dan's room.

"There's a reason for a single room," he explained carefully.

She sat down on the end of the bed, crossing her arms. "I'm sure there is," she agreed.

"We're suppose to be married," he reminded her.

"Don't you think you're carrying this game a little too far? If you want me to sleep with you, Dan, all you have to do is ask."

He'd opened his mouth to protest her first question, when the following statement caught him off guard. "Would you?" he asked with interest.

She eyed him thoughtfully. "Probably." She held up her hand in a warning gesture. "After we know each other better. I don't know what type of woman you're used to, but I don't go for recreational sex."

He was admittedly relieved, despite experiencing a slight stab of disappointment. He hadn't planned on forcing her, or anything like that, but if she'd showed the slightest inclination in making love with him, he sure wasn't stupid enough to turn it down.

"I never thought you did, Jenny," he answered honestly.

She smiled, leaning back on her elbows. Dan tried not to notice how the gesture pulled the material tight against her breasts. Nothing about this was going to be easy, he decided.

"Tell me why you're so determined to put our self-control to this test," she instructed.

"In case it's slipped that rather vague memory of yours, there's someone or several someones out there who don't want you to tell your story. They've already drugged you, probably run you off the highway, and we have no way of knowing what they'll try next. You'd make a lovely corpse, sweetheart, but I'm a hell of a lot more interested in keeping you alive."

At his harsh, gritty tone, she turned a little pale and Dan felt a momentary pang of regret that he laid it on the line so graphically. But damn it, he was working in the dark, and until she could shed some light on this situation, he'd be as cautious as necessary.

She lay back on the mattress, closing her eyes as she

rubbed her temples wearily with her fingertips. "Why can't I remember?" she whispered.

He sat down beside her, stroking her bangs away from her forehead. The doctor had removed the heavy bandage before discharging her, and the only sign of the accident was a dark row of stitches over her right eye. She'd worried about that, but the doctor had assured her the scar would fade in time. Dan had told her she looked dashing, kind of like a female pirate.

"I've been thinking about that," he admitted. "It's odd that your memory is so spotty. For instance, you remembered seeing me in the airport, right down to what I was reading."

She didn't open her eyes. "That naked lady on the cover is hard to forget. Not to mention the size of that diamond. It looked like something Elizabeth Taylor would wear."

"It was the Princess Carlotta diamond," he said nonsensically, trying not to bend down and crush her pink lips.

"What?"

He shook his head. "Never mind. Anyway, how can you remember choosing me to help you, but not why you needed help in the first place?"

"That feels so good," she murmured as his fingers continued their gentle stroking. "For your information, I remember everything about you."

"But that doesn't make sense."

She opened her eyes and the message in their smooth chocolate depths sent a thrill coursing through him. "Yes, it does. To me, anyway."

Dan allowed himself to drown in their warmth for a long, silent moment, feeling attraction and something more. He had to struggle against the tides that were drawing him away from his initial purpose.

Forcing a shaky laugh, he suddenly stood, breaking their intense eye contact. With his hands jammed into his back pockets, he walked over to the window, gazing blindly down into the parking lot.

"We'd better take you back to the hospital. Because there's something definitely wrong with your head."

"No, there's something wrong with my heart," she answered with unnerving honesty. "I've never felt like this about anyone before, Dan."

He couldn't allow himself to turn and look at those soft, beautiful eyes he could feel directed at his back. "That's probably because you've never had anyone try to kill you before. Danger is a powerful aphrodisiac."

"I suppose so," she murmured thoughtfully. "You've probably discovered that once or twice."

"Yeah," he mumbled, knowing that much to be true.

He neglected to add that those random occasions had contributed to some very enjoyable sex, but they'd been rash whirlwinds of passion. Jenny, on the other hand, made him feel as if he were slowly sinking in quicksand.

"I thought so." She sounded sad, and a little hurt.

Dan forced himself to return to the initial point of the conversation. "Look, it's crossed my mind that you've suddenly realized how serious this all is and you're afraid to remember. I have a feeling that when this all started out, the idea of danger gave you kind of a kinky thrill."

She sat up against the headboard, eyeing him with newfound respect. "That's very perceptive. I think you may be right."

"What do you do for a living?" he asked, suddenly realizing she'd never volunteered the information and he'd been too stupid to ask. That was probably the damn key and it had been under his nose the entire time!

"I'm an architect."

"You're kidding."

That wasn't what he'd been expecting. He'd thought she

was going to tell him she was involved in politics, or the government. After all, she'd said this story went all the way to Washington, D.C.

"I have my own firm in San Francisco. I started out doing mostly remodeling jobs—restoring Victorian town houses, that type of thing. But the last few years things have taken off and I've been getting more and more commercial buildings. In fact, I've just taken on a partner."

She smiled, and as Dan wondered if the idea of her partner caused that light to gleam in her dark eyes, he felt unreasonably jealous.

"It sounds as if you enjoy your work," he probed carefully.

"I do. In fact, it's one of my great passions."

"I see," he said noncommittally, not really understanding at all.

"There's something incredibly exciting about watching something I've created in my mind become a reality—a beautiful tower of glass and steel reaching up toward the sky. I suppose it's my way of leaving a mark on the world. I love knowing that my buildings will still be standing there long after I'm gone," she admitted somewhat self-consciously.

"Or at least until the next earthquake hits."

She wrinkled her nose in a gesture he found out of character, but endearing all the same. Jenny was an odd combination of practicality and romanticism, Dan decided, growing more bewitched with every passing moment.

"That's not a nice thing to point out," she scolded lightly. "You know those signs next to the scanners in airports that warn about bomb jokes being taken very seriously?"

"I've seen them."

"That's how we San Franciscans feel about earthquake jokes."

"You know, I really do think you like the fantasy of living dangerously," he accused.

Jenny smiled. "You may just have a point there, McGee," she admitted with a light sigh. "That's probably what got me into this mess in the first place."

Then her expression turned sober. The bantering was over and a note of uncertainty crept into her voice. "Speaking of that, what do you suggest I do now?"

He'd been giving it a great deal of thought himself. "Tomorrow we'll drive back to the city and drop by your office. Something there might stimulate your memory."

"We?"

Dan's blue eyes shone with a sudden intensity. "You didn't pick yourself up any transitory white knight, Jenny. We're in this together."

She looked relieved, but her eyes showed her concern. "What about your own work? You must have been booked on that flight for some reason."

Dan had almost forgotten his story on governmental graft, but it no longer seemed all that earth-shattering. Not compared to Jenny Winslow's problem. Besides, crooked senators had been around long before he'd started banging away on a typewriter and they'd still be doing their dirty deeds after he retired to stay home and play with his grandchildren. The story could wait.

"Don't worry about it." He waved her concern away with his hand. "*Newsview* knows I'll deliver. I always have."

Her fond look melted his bones. "That I can well believe, McGee. I'm still thanking my lucky stars that you were in that terminal."

Eat your heart out, Max, old boy, Dan thought with a bold, inward smile.

Chapter Four

Not unexpectedly, Jenny ran down like an overwound alarm clock shortly after their conversation. Dan sat in a chair a few feet from the bed, watching with concern as the color slowly faded from her face.

"You need a nap," he finally said.

"I've been sleeping almost around the clock," she argued with halfhearted resistance. "Besides, I haven't taken a nap since I was six months old."

"Don't argue. You'll be able to remember things better once you're well rested. Besides, we're leaving first thing tomorrow morning."

"Did you say we were driving?"

"I think that's best, don't you? There's always the chance someone's watching the airports. At this point, we don't even know who to look out for."

Dan was beginning to hate this situation. It gave him the eerie sense of walking through one of those haunted houses at an amusement park. You knew there were all sorts of things just waiting to jump out at you, but you never knew when or where they'd hit.

Her brown eyes showed worry and an obvious regret. "I'm sorry," she murmured, her fingers plucking at the bed-spread.

"Don't be. It's not your fault you've forgotten. The doctor said it was a normal result of your injury."

Jenny's gaze was directed downward and she was obviously uncomfortable. "That's not what I was talking about," she said softly. She slowly lifted her head, her eyes displaying a deep, private pain. "I'm sorry about getting you mixed up in all this."

"Don't talk like that," he demanded gruffly. "You didn't get me mixed up in anything. I volunteered every step of the way, and if you haven't figured that out yet, you've got a lot more wrong with your head than a lapse in memory and a few stitches."

He lit a cigarette and began to pace the floor in long, angry strides, trying to work off his frustration. He stopped in front of the window, looking out onto the parking lot again, watching the cars come and go. Two men in dark suits entered the front doors. Were they the ones? Or the college-age kid in red shorts and running shoes; was he jogging from hotel to hotel, looking for a vulnerable, single woman?

As he watched the steady stream of guests, Dan realized he'd never once considered the fact that Jenny might technically be on the wrong side, that whatever she'd been doing might be illegal. It wouldn't matter, he decided. It would just make things a little stickier.

Dan couldn't remember ever being so intrigued by a woman; he'd never wanted anyone as much as he wanted Jenny. Not the type to deal in self-deception, he knew the man he faced in the mirror each morning when he shaved was no Tom Selleck. Yet women invariably found him appealing and his sex life was both interesting and varied. He was an honest man, always pointing out that his current life-style made a long-term relationship impractical, if not impossible, and it had never been a disadvantage.

Once, six years ago, he'd been close to marriage, only to have the woman leave him without a backward glance for a Saudi Arabian sheik. Dan's ardor was no match for a fleet of oil tankers and it had taught him an important lesson about this new breed of liberated women who were unable, or unwilling, to offer emotional commitment. He took what life had to offer and when it was time to move on, neither party had any regrets.

A nagging little thought teased his mind that once all this was over and he moved on, he'd miss Jenny very, very much. He wondered if, by any wild stretch of the imagination, she might feel the same way. Dan believed what she'd said about not entering into casual sex; for Jenny Winslow to go to bed with a man, she might not have to love him, but there'd have to be some strong bond. That brought an unwelcome thought and he turned slowly, his eyes meeting hers in an intense, unwavering gaze.

"I want to ask you something."

She nodded, her expression solemn as she took in the harsh lines of his face.

"Are you married?"

"No."

"Are you sure? Maybe that's something else you've forgotten."

"I'd never forget that," she contradicted calmly. Her smooth brow furrowed and he watched her unconscious grimace as the stitches pulled. "Would it make a difference?"

Would it? he asked himself, knowing the answer instantly. He stubbed out the cigarette and crossed the room, coming to stand in front of her. Reaching down, he combed his fingers through her thick, honey-blond hair, pushing it back from her face.

"Not one bit. I only wanted to know if there was an irate

husband out there who was going to beat the hell out of me for spending the night with his wife."

His hands moved down the slender column of her throat, resting lightly on her shoulders. She was far tenser than her expression would indicate, and his fingers began a gentle massage.

"Not that it wouldn't be worth it, you understand," he continued, his deep voice husky with pent-up desire. "I'd be willing to take on an entire battalion for you, Jenny."

She had shut her eyes to his intimate gaze, and Dan saw tears welling underneath her long lashes. She suddenly looked lost and a little forlorn.

"Oh, Dan," she whispered, "I don't want you to have to do that."

He had never felt more helpless in his life as he dropped down next to her on the bed, bringing her into the circle of his arms. She buried her head in his shoulder and her anguished sobs tore at his heart. He rocked her gently, crooning soft, inarticulate words of comfort as the afternoon sun slanted lower through the window.

Finally she stopped, sniffling slightly as she scrubbed her wet cheeks with the back of her hand. Dan knew the chances of finding a clean handkerchief in any of his pockets were nonexistent, and he left her for a moment to retrieve the box of Kleenex from the bathroom.

"Thank you." She managed a watery smile. "I'm sorry. I never cry; really I don't."

Dan believed it. He shrugged, taking the tissue from her trembling hand to dry the sparkling tears from her skin.

"Hey, you're entitled. You've been through a lot. Now will you agree to take that nap?"

She nodded. "That's probaby a good idea. I'm suddenly very tired." Her fingers smoothed the knit skirt. "But I can't sleep in this."

Dan moved to the closet, extracting a long, white cotton nightgown.

"Another souvenir from my shopping trip," he explained at her surprised glance. "You can either change into this, or just sleep in that lacy thing."

"I think I'll sleep in the teddy and save the nightgown for tonight," she decided. "Wearing a night-gown in the middle of the day will make me feel like I'm sick." Dan watched her inner strength returning. "Not only do I never cry. I never get sick."

"A tower of steel," he teased, his laughing gaze turning serious as a deathly pallor fell across her face. "Jenny? What's the matter?"

She was staring far beyond him and Dan turned, seeing nothing but the door behind him.

"Jenny?" he asked again softly, waving his hand in front of her face.

She slowly returned her attention to him, her expression haunted. Her hands trembled in her lap and Dan caught them in his, shocked by their icy feel.

"I almost remembered." Her low, labored words sounded like she was speaking from the bottom of the sea. "It was right there, right in front of me . . ." Her shoulders slumped as she shook her head. "But I couldn't quite see it. It was so close."

"It's okay," he assured her, his fingers busy at the gold buckle on her dress. "Don't you see, Jenny? This is good news."

Her hand momentarily covered his. "Good news?"

"Your memory's not permanently wiped out. It's there, just waiting for you to recall it. All you have to do is relax. And get enough rest," he tacked on pointedly, lifting her hand and putting it back on her lap while he unbuckled her belt.

"Is that why you're undressing me? For a nap?"

"Of course!" Grievance laced his tone. "What did you think?"

She gave him a ghost of a smile that didn't quite reach her eyes. "I thought perhaps you were going to take advantage of my weakened state and ravish me while I couldn't resist."

"That's ridiculous," he snapped. "Lift up your arms." He brought the pink dress up over her head. "I'd never do a thing like that," he complained as he pulled back the bed covers.

"I know," she sighed, slipping between the sheets.

Dan thought he detected just the hint of regret in her tone and smiled. It was nice to know he wasn't the only one who wished the other would make the first serious move. The only problem was, until all this was settled, he wasn't sure the time would ever be right.

The sun sank into an unseen horizon as Dan sat in silence, reflecting on their situation. He wondered if he was going to be able to keep her safe without any outside help. But whatever she'd been involved in, Jenny had obviously had her own reasons not to trust anyone else with her secret. If it were cut and dried, wouldn't she have gone to the police?

He lit a cigarette as he mentally kicked himself for not thinking of one obvious trail earlier today. Dusk had fallen; the room was cast in long gray shadows and he knew it was too late to call New York. The records at *Newsview* magazine were a gold mine of information. Maybe, just maybe, the computer would connect Jenny with someone who could provide a clue.

"Dan?" She was sitting up, pushing clouds of tumbled hair out of her eyes, trying to locate him in the dark.

He reached out, flicking on the soft glow of the table lamp. "Right here," he assured her.

Relief flooded her features. "I'm acting like a ninny, aren't I?"

"Only when you ask dumb questions like that," he countered. "How do you feel?"

She managed a smile. "Rested. But my hair is all gummy." She brought a handful in front of her face, eyeing it with disdain.

"I suppose it must be," he agreed. "After all, your head was bleeding, then they put all that antiseptic on it. Some of that stuff was bound to get into your hair." Dan belatedly realized this was nothing to tell a lady concerned about her appearance. "It looks fine, though."

"Liar." She pushed the sheet away, swinging her legs around to put her feet on the floor. "I'm going to wash it."

He was on his own feet in an instant, blocking her way to the bathroom. "The hell you are."

She tilted her chin, meeting his gaze bravely. "Please move out of my way, McGee. If I'm going to die, I want to go out with shiny hair."

"That isn't very goddamn funny!" he roared suddenly.

By her own stricken expression, Jennifer appeared to share his feelings. "I'm sorry. It was meant to be a joke, but it came off a little flat, didn't it?"

"Don't joke about that, Jenny," he warned.

She put her hand on his arm, her warm brown gaze moving tenderly over his face. "I'm sorry. But I *am* going to wash my hair."

He muttered a low, harsh oath. "Are you always this stubborn?"

"So I've been told."

"You've got stitches."

She lifted her hand to her forehead. "I know. They hurt."

"So you probably shouldn't be washing your hair."

"I'll be careful."

"If your actions so far indicate your idea of caution, sweetheart, I'm not letting you under that shower."

"Dan." Her voice turned maple-syrup rich and her fingers stroked his forearm. "Please let's not fight like this."

He sighed, knowing when he was licked. His mind whirled, attempting to come up with a compromise. "I'll wash it for you."

"I don't know," she replied hesitantly.

"It'll dry by morning, if that's what you're worried about."

She eyed him thoughtfully. "If I give in to a momentary weakness and change my mind about making love to you, do you promise you won't take me up on it?"

He groaned. "Come on, Jenny, I'm only human. What do you want, a saint?"

She thought about that a moment. "You've got a point," she admitted, crossing her arms over the lacy bodice of her teddy. "I guess I'll just have to wash it myself."

He fought down the irritation he felt by the fact that Jenny was suddenly the one making demands. What the hell would Max Harte do now?

"You know, I could refuse to let you wash your hair in the first place."

She met his flashing gaze with a level one of her own. "You'd have to tie me down first. And you'd never do that."

He crossed his arms over his own chest, glaring down at her. "Want to make a bet?"

Dan gave Jenny points for fortitude as her self-satisfied expression wavered only slightly. "You're a bully."

"That's what they always say about us big guys when we try to stand up for our rights," he agreed cheerfully.

She looked at him suspiciously. "Would you really tie me up?"

"You can put it to the test, if you like."

"I'd scream."

"There's always adhesive tape."

Her complexion darkened with an angry flush. "You wouldn't dare!"

He shrugged uncaringly. "Why not? It's a more proven method of shutting up bossy females than some others I've tried over the years."

Her eyes narrowed. "You're putting me on. I know you are."

He merely shrugged again. Of course he was, but he was afraid that if he let Jenny walk all over him on this one, she might get too cocky and end up putting them in danger. She had to learn that once in a while it didn't hurt to let someone else make the decisions. Dan had complied with that cloak-and-dagger routine in the airport; he hadn't insisted she tell him what she was doing on the plane, and by his acquiescence to her wishes, she'd almost been killed. No, from now on, she'd have to understand that he was the one calling the shots.

"All right," she agreed finally. "If you insist, I'll let you wash my hair."

"Thank you."

She nodded, brushing past him with an amazingly haughty attitude for one who'd been sobbing her heart out a few hours earlier.

"You're welcome." She looked back over her shoulder. "Well, are you coming?"

The minute Dan entered the small bathroom, he knew he'd be in trouble if he stepped into that shower with her.

"I've got another idea," he suggested, "it's a deep sink; we can wash it that way."

Jenny's relieved expression indicated she'd been suffering the same trepidation. "Now that's the best idea you've come up with all day," she admitted with a smile.

"Mmm," she murmured later as his fingertips massaged her scalp. "For a big man, Dan McGee, you've got marvelously gentle hands."

As his fingers tangled in the long, wet strands of her hair, Dan tried to keep his mind on the task at hand. He warned himself not to look down, to keep his gaze directed on her shampoo-covered head, but he was only a man, and the temptation was too great.

The red globe of the heat lamp overhead cast a crimson glow to her satiny flesh and the teddy clung to her in a way that was anything but calming. The way it rose up over her curves as she bent over the sink wasn't any help, either.

"I think I made a hell of a mistake," he said under his breath as he rinsed the green herbal shampoo from her hair. He had been speaking more to himself than to Jenny, but she heard him just the same.

She opened her eyes, turning around to look up at him with an unabashed desire that threatened to crumble the fragile parapets of his resolve.

"Dan," she whispered on a soft breath that was part request, part demurral.

"I've got to kiss you, Jenny," he said on a ragged groan. "I'll go crazy if I don't."

Jenny's lips trembled under the touch of his thumb at the corner of her mouth. When she pressed her palm against his chest, Dan knew she could feel the already wildly erratic beat of his heart accelerate at her touch.

Dan warned himself to go gently, that Jenny had already suffered too many shocks in the last two days. While his body ached with unsatiated need and he wanted nothing more than to carry her into the other room and make love to her until neither of them could move, he knew restraint was in order.

With a muffled sigh, his lips covered hers in a touch that

was infinitely tender, remarkably controlled. Dan forced himself to use only the softest pressure, drawing out the kiss for a magic moment that transcended the realm of normal time and space. His lips feathered a path from one corner of her lips to the center and she sighed blissfully as he repeated the evocative path from the other corner with soft, tantalizing caresses.

"Open your mouth, Jenny," he murmured, drinking in her soft breath. "Let me taste you, sweetheart."

She answered with a low, lingering moan, meeting his request. At the same time her hands slowly crawled up his chest, across the wide expanse of his shoulders, her fingers linking behind his neck as she fit herself against him. Dan felt her swelling breasts under the silky fabric convey a firm and welcoming invitation and realized that if he didn't back away from this delicious temptation right now, it would be too late.

Slowly, regretfully, he took her hands from around his neck, suffering a loss throughout every pulsating nerve in his body. "You are definitely living dangerously."

With a muffled sigh he twisted off the water and pulled down a big, fluffy white towel which he wrapped around her head. "We'd better get out of here and order some dinner before I forget I'm suppose to be playing the part of a gentleman."

Jenny nodded slowly, her own eyes dark with desire as she struggled to return to reality. Finally, she sighed, going up on her toes to press a brief kiss against his lips. A bolt of lightning seared its way down his spine.

"I suppose you're right; thank you, Dan. I knew you were a man I could trust."

"Yeah," he muttered, "A real teddy bear."

"I like teddy bears." She reached out, squeezing his hand with an affectionate, reassuring gesture. "And I like you."

"Get dressed," he instructed gruffly, trying to keep a curb on his own hunger.

She stopped momentarily in the doorway. "When you start throwing your weight around, McGee, you sound more like a gruff old bear just waking up after a long cold winter," she teased. "But I still think it's all an act."

"Just don't push your luck, sweetheart," he muttered as she left the room.

Rubbing his hand over the dark stubble of his cheek, Dan decided a shave was in order before dinner. As he spread the hot, creamy lather over his face, he wondered why he was even trying to impress her. Women like Jenny Winslow might be willing to fool around with guys like him, but when it came to a permanent relationship, she'd marry someone like herself. Some guy who wore three-piece suits and knotted his ties with perfect Windsors. Probably that partner she had smiled about, he decided, wielding his razor with careless strokes as an unwelcome burst of jealousy seared through him.

Chapter Five

Jenny had already changed into the long, white nightgown and was seated cross-legged on the bed, reading the room service menu, when Dan came out of the bathroom.

"Good heavens," she remarked, looking up at his face. "What did you do to yourself?"

"Dull blade," he grunted, knowing he must look like an idiot with pieces of toilet paper stuck to his ravaged skin. He wasn't about to admit to the uncharacteristic jealousy that had caused him to hack up his face.

"Well, at least now we're a match." At his questioning look, she elaborated. "Now we both look as if we've been in an accident."

Dan didn't want to talk about that subject, either. "Anything good in there?"

She shrugged. "Just the typical room service fare."

"You haven't eaten since breakfast," he remembered belatedly.

"My throat was too sore to think about eating earlier," she assured him. Then her eyes brightened with a mischievous light. "Besides, you took my mind off food entirely."

"You keep asking for it, sweetheart," he warned, pulling on a pair of clean shorts under the towel, "and you may just end up getting more than you bargained for."

"Keep that thought," she murmured, one pink-tipped fingernail caught thoughtfully between her lips.

Dan had never given a great deal of consideration to men's underwear, finding far more pleasure in the lacy secrets women wore under their clothes. But he suddenly wished he was wearing something sexier than the blue boxers he'd just put on. Some silky bikini briefs, maybe, a blazing crimson color.

Her steady, silent gaze was making his nerves scream, but Dan managed to maintain an aura of masculine nonchalance as he pulled a pair of faded jeans and a shirt out of his suitcase.

"I'll bet you're one of those people who never unpack, no matter how long you're in a hotel," Jenny observed with uncanny accuracy.

"Bull's eye. While you, on the other hand, can't relax until everything's neatly put into its assigned place."

"Bingo," she agreed cheerfully. "You work surrounded by papers spread over every flat surface, including the floor. Yet out of all that absolute chaos comes tight, succinct prose capable of winning a Pulitzer. It's probably the closest thing in the journalism world to a twentieth-century miracle."

She was right, of course.

"I'll bet your office could pass for a hospital operating room," he countered. "It's brightly lit, the furniture is functionally spartan, and your pristine drafting board is never cluttered. You keep your pencils in a holder, their points always sharpened, and the tips of your pens are never globbed with ink."

Dan wondered what kind of masochist he'd become that he kept actively looking for differences between them.

"You've been spying on me," Jenny accused with a smile. She chewed thoughtfully on her fingernail, fixing him with an appraising gaze as she continued the game.

"If those French fries were any example, you survive on fast food, although I'd bet your favorite dinner is a slab of barely cooked red meat, mounds of mashed potatoes, salad, and green peas. All washed down with a tall, foamy draft beer."

"What kind of dressing?" he challenged.

"Thousand Island," she replied without missing a beat.

"Got it on the first try." He pulled on the jeans. "Let's see, what does the lady prefer?" He rubbed his battered chin thoughtfully. "Your favorite San Francisco restaurant is an intimate little French place, unknown to tourists, where the maitre'd knows all the clientele by name. It's a traditional enough place that the waiters wear tuxedos, but modern enough that the lady isn't given a menu without prices listed, because that would offend your ideas about women's equality."

She brought her knees up against her chest, lowering her chin to them. "So far, so good," she answered. "Keep going."

Dan put on the shirt, leaving it hanging open as he came to stand over her. "Normally, you're a vegetarian, because you don't believe in eating anything that could have children."

She grinned and Dan knew he'd hit close to home. "However, on occasion, if the gentleman you're with is one of those queasy types who cringes at eating something he has to step over on the sidewalk, you'll order escargot."

"Why would I do that?" she challenged, her eyes dancing.

"Because deep down you're a rebel. I suspect you're the most unruly when you're out with a man who's a mirror image of that sophisticated, poised facade you've worked so hard to create for yourself."

She didn't answer, but by the slight flush on her cheeks,

Dan knew he was batting a thousand. "You always order California wines, but you're so charming in your little rebellion that the haughty French waiter never lifts a disapproving brow."

"That's very perceptive of you," she acknowledged softly. "I'm impressed."

"Oh, I've got your number, Jenny Winslow. So don't try to get away with anything."

"My number?"

"You get a kick out of shocking people by discarding that sophisticated attitude you wear like a second skin when they least expect it. You'd probably drive the average man to drink, just trying to keep up with your quick mood changes."

Her eyes met his in a softly challengingly way. "But you're not the average man, are you, McGee?"

He took a moment to answer, fighting against the message he read in her eyes. Dan felt as if he were drowning in deep pools of hot chocolate.

"I like to think I'm not," he agreed, his casual tone taking a Herculean effort. He picked up the menu from the mattress. "Ready to order?"

"Mmm," she breathed, her gaze slowly moving over his bare chest.

Dan had looked at women in this same suggestive manner, but he'd never had the tables turned on him like Jenny was doing now. It unsettled and excited him at the same time and it took all the self-control he could muster to call in their dinner order. As the conversation turned to impersonal small talk while they waited for the room service waiter, Dan wondered how he was ever going to survive this forced proximity without spending the entire night under a cold shower.

"That was delicious." Jenny finished the last of her fettucini, leaning back in the chair with a happy sigh.

Having finished his steak long ago, Dan had enjoyed watching Jenny's undisguised enthusiasm as she enjoyed her meal. She'd single-handedly made a spinach salad, fettucini, two pieces of French bread, half a carafe of white wine, and two cups of coffee disappear. Not to mention an enormous piece of Black Forest cake.

"Another secret passion," she admitted, wiping a smudge of fudge frosting off her lips with the tip of her tongue. Dan had to stifle a groan at her provocative gesture. "I'm an absolute fiend about chocolate."

Despite her slender frame, she certainly wasn't a picky eater. He liked that in a woman. Of course, he'd yet to find anything he didn't like about Jenny Winslow. That, too, was a surprise. Usually by now little habits would begin to grate on his nerves.

"So the way to the lady's heart is through her stomach?" He vowed to buy a five pound box of chocolates the minute they got back to the city.

She smiled softly. "That's one way."

Her eyes were lit once again with that unspoken message, but Dan decided it was better left unanswered for the moment. "So," he stated with undue casualness, "did you always want to be an architect?"

Jenny's expression revealed that she recognized his ploy to change the subject and appreciated it. They were walking a delicate tightrope between desire and common sense and it was getting slipperier with each passing moment.

"Always, from the time I received my first box of blocks. While all the other girls were busy designing clothes for their Barbie Dolls, I was designing highrises. It seems to be in my blood."

Dan could certainly understand that. He felt the same

way about his career; he couldn't remember not wanting to write. "Is either one of your parents an architect?"

She frowned slightly, the furrows marring her smooth forehead. "No."

He wondered what he'd said wrong. "I'm sorry. You just mentioned it being in your blood, and I thought—"

She shook her head, remaining silent as she stared out at the sparkling lights of Sacramento. Not wanting to press the point, Dan busied himself by moving the portable table out into the hallway. He returned to stand over her, his fingers lightly massaging her shoulders. She was so tense.

"Jenny? Did I say something wrong?"

She exhaled a weary sigh, reaching up to cover his hand with her own. "No. My family just isn't one of my favorite topics."

"Oh." A small, significant little silence settled over them.

"It isn't that I don't love them," she said finally, speaking as much to herself as to him. "My family owns a ranch in southern Oregon. It's been in our family for three generations. I was supposed to make it a fourth."

"But you're not into cattle," he prompted when she fell silent again.

She managed a slight grin. "Why do you think I'm a vegetarian? Eighteen years of living with all those Black Angus would convert anyone to tofu and bean sprouts."

He shrugged. "So, you're not into a home on the range. That might have come as a disappointment, but certainly your parents couldn't blame you for having other goals."

She gave him a long, pointed look. "When you work a ranch, McGee, you don't worry about other goals or what makes you happy," she said firmly, as if quoting a doctrine she'd heard too often while growing up. "You think about work and responsibility."

She laughed then, a short, bitter sound that Dan hated to

hear coming from her. "Daddy once told me that if all I wanted out of life was to be happy, then I should just run off and be a hippie. If I wanted to be his daughter, then I'd settle down and marry Jimmy Morgan and worry about being a good wife and mother."

"Jimmy Morgan?" Dan knew it was irrational of him to hate the guy. After all, if Jenny had felt anything for him, she'd be somewhere up in the Cascade Mountains right now, tending babies and herding cattle. As vivid an imagination as Dan possessed, he couldn't envision that particular scenario.

"Jimmy's parents owned the adjoining ranch. He was four years older than I was and both families expected us to get married and join the two properties."

"Did anyone ever bother to ask you or Jimmy?"

She shrugged. "It was just decided when I was born; I think they all considered it a self-fulfilling prophecy."

"You didn't love him?"

"I loved him as a friend and the big brother I never had. But I certainly couldn't have married him, even if I'd wanted to stay in the valley. Which I didn't."

"What about him? What did he think about this master plan for your lives?"

Her fingers twisted nervously in her lap. "Jimmy was a little more easygoing than me," she stated noncommittally.

Jimmy Morgan had obviously loved Jenny, an idea Dan didn't find all that surprising. "Which means he went along with the idea, but you raised bloody hell."

She gave him a slight smile. "You hit the nail on the head when you called me a rebel. In the eighteen years I lived at home, my parents and I never agreed on anything. I didn't want to fight all the time, but they couldn't understand that I wanted more excitement from life than they did . . ."

Her voice wavered a little and she sighed deeply. "Mama accused me of giving Daddy his heart attack."

"I don't think that's possible," Dan said carefully as he felt the renewed tensing of her shoulders under his fingertips.

He was suddenly more appreciative of his own mother. Although Lillian was not the type who volunteered to be a Cub Scout den mother, she'd always believed individuals had to follow their own star. As both she and his father had done with mixed results.

Jenny's slim shoulder drooped. "I know. But when I was younger, it scared me enough that I gave in and agreed to marry Jimmy."

Dan stiffened. "You said you weren't married."

She turned toward him, her expression displaying surprise at his gritty tone. "I know. And I'm not."

"Oh."

"Don't tell me you're jealous, Dan McGee?" she asked incredulously.

"Hell, no," he lied quickly. "I just like to know what I'm getting into. We're already working in the dark; I don't want to run into any irate spouses you may have out there."

Her slender face was sober. "I knew in my heart that if I married Jimmy it would never work. I wanted to be an architect in the big city; I wanted to travel. He was content to stay home and raise cattle."

"Nothing wrong with raising cattle," Dan felt obliged to point out, personally grateful someone was willing to supply him with a steady diet of hamburgers and steaks.

"Of course not," she countered, "if it's what you want to do. That's what Jimmy wanted to do. I couldn't understand why he was allowed to be happy, while I was suppose to sacrifice everything just because I was a woman."

"I can understand your problem with that reasoning," he

agreed, once again thinking of Lillian McGee. If anyone had ever made the mistake of telling his mother there was something she couldn't do because of her sex, he knew she would have laughed and proceeded to do it anyway.

"So," Jenny continued her story, "I tried to tell myself that getting married was probably like going to the dentist; when it was all over, it wouldn't be nearly as bad as I anticipated."

She grinned suddenly, her face lighting up the room like a thousand-watt light bulb. Dan watched the little imps dancing in her dark eyes and knew that she must have driven her conservative rancher parents crazy from time to time. But what they'd obviously considered a distressing bent toward nonconformity, Dan found entrancing.

"But when the minister asked me to repeat the vows, I just couldn't say them. I apologized to Jimmy and ran out of the church, then jumped into his car and drove straight to the bus depot."

"You ran away in your wedding dress?"

"My luggage hadn't been put into the car yet, and I didn't dare go home," she pointed out. "Besides, when I arrived in San Francisco, hardly anyone gave me a second glance."

That he could well believe. "So what happened then?"

She shrugged. "Jimmy was a better sport than my parents. After I called to explain, he put my clothes on the next bus." Her eyes grew a little moist at the distant memory. "He even loaned me some money to get started. I got a room, a job, and went to school at night."

"You put yourself through college? All by yourself?"

"The experience was good for me; it taught me to be independent."

"I should think so," he murmured. "My mother is going to love you," he stated suddenly, as if taking her home to meet Lillian was a foregone conclusion. Dan hadn't consciously thought of it, but as he heard himself saying the words, he knew it was what he wanted to do.

Jenny glanced at him with interest. "Why?"

"Because you're soul mates," he stated, pressing his lips against the top of her head. Her hair smelled fresh, like a forest after a spring rain. God, how he wanted her!

"Tell me about your family," she instructed, genuinely interested.

Dan's eyes moved over her uplifted face, taking in the purple shadows under her eyes. The rosy color that had been the result of rest and a good meal was fading and she looked tired.

"Some other time," he instructed firmly. "You need to get some sleep if we're going to leave first thing in the morning."

She nodded her acquiescence. "All right. But don't get the idea you're going to get away with bossing me around all the time like this, McGee. Once I get back on my feet, this is going to be a fifty-fifty proposition."

"Think you're capable of keeping up?"

She laughed. "I know I am. Get ready for a few surprises," she warned.

Dan knew that was no idle threat. Jenny Winslow had given him one surprise after another since the moment she'd walked up to him, claimed to be his wife, and tipped his world on its axis.

He lay in bed, puzzling over the changes Jenny had already brought to his life. Dan couldn't remember a time he'd been willing to drop an assignment without so much as a backward glance. It was more than her promise of a great story; he knew that whatever else he did with his life, nothing would ever be as important as protecting Jenny.

A necessary trait developed during his life as a journalistic gypsy was the ability to fall asleep whenever the opportunity presented itself. In fact, on rare occasions, he'd been known to sleep standing up, braced against a wall, a tree, or whatever was handy. Yet tonight thoughts of Jenny poked and probed, keeping sleep at arm's length. Even when drowsiness did finally steal over him, dreams of her in a never-ending variety of dangers tortured his mind.

Finally, one particularly frightening nightmare jerked him from the edge of sleep while the room was still draped in the shadows of early dawn. He lay on his back as his mind whirled with a kaleidoscope of questions and possible explanations. Jenny was always at the center, appearing in a dazzling variety of moods and scenarios, none of which he could piece together into a workable whole. There were a myriad of facets to Jenny Winslow and, try as he might, he couldn't make sense out of any of them.

Deciding to put away that unconstructive behavior, he cast a glance at the clock radio beside the bed, noting that the *Newsview* offices in New York would be open. He pulled back the covers carefully as he left the bed, not wanting to wake her as he made his way to the well-equipped bathroom that boasted a wall telephone.

His nerves on edge, he smoked two cigarettes as he waited for the research librarian to locate Jennifer Winslow in the data banks of the computer file. When she finally popped up, Dan was stunned into silence.

"You've got the wrong file," he stated categorically.

"I don't think so," Marge Hendershot, *Newsview's* most efficient research librarian replied. "Hold on, Dan, and let me call it up again." There was a momentary silence from the other end of the phone and Dan waited impatiently, knowing that for probably the first time in her highly efficient career, the woman had made a mistake.

"Nope," she said, as if answering his unspoken accusation, "this is the right file."

"It can't be," Dan argued. "Jennifer Winslow." He slowly spelled her last name for clarification. "She's an architect with a small company in San Francisco. She restores Victorian houses."

"She obviously does a lot more than that," Marge countered. "The lady's passport must have more pages than *War and Peace.*"

"Look," Dan said slowly, his mind trying to make some sense out of Marge's information, "we're obviously talking about two different Jennifer Winslows. If you get time today, try cross-referencing that file. There's got to be a snafu somewhere."

"If there is, Dan McGee, the mix-up is on your end. Not mine." Marge considered her library inviolate.

"Probably so, darlin'," he drawled obligingly, "but will you be a sweetheart and check it out anyway?"

"Do I get lunch next time you're in town?"

Dan almost smiled. "Marge, if you can come up with anything that explains this unexpected turn of events, you can have whatever your sweet little heart desires."

She chuckled, a husky, lascivious sound. "Honey, if I were to get what I'd really like from you, I'd put a thirty-year marriage in jeopardy. I think we'd better stick to lunch."

The two had been friends for a long time, and Dan usually enjoyed these conversations, but this morning he was unable to rise to her teasing innuendos.

"Thanks," he said absently, trying to sort her information out in his mind. "I'll call you back."

"Sure," she agreed, the question mark in her voice displaying her curiosity at his uncharacteristic behavior. "Bye."

Forgetting to answer, he hung up, lighting yet another

cigarette as he sat in frowning silence, smoking and reflecting on their situation.

When he finally exited the bathroom, Jenny was awake, hitching herself up in the bed.

"Good morning."

"You haven't exactly been straight with me, have you, Jenny?" he asked without preamble.

She stared at him, her smile wavering as she took in his grim expression. "Straight with you? What are you talking about?"

"That nice little architectural business—the one that's growing enough for you to take on a partner? That's a bit of an understatement, isn't it?"

As he watched her carefully, a fleeting shadow darkened her eyes. She didn't quite meet his unwavering gaze. "I *did* take on a partner."

It was her tone that shook him more than her words. Dan knew for a fact that she'd just handed him a cozy little half-truth. He experienced the disquieting thought that he'd been taken for a fool.

"Oh, I'm willing to believe that. My only question is, which of you is going to handle all that overseas work?"

Her head came up defiantly and Dan caught a new, stiffer note in her voice he'd never heard before. "You've been spying on me."

"I wasn't spying on you, damn it! I was trying to help, but I can't if you're not honest with me."

She gave a small, uncaring shrug. "So I've done a little foreign work. What does that have to do with you? With us?"

"A *little?* Is that what you call it? When the hell do you have time to restore those quaint Victorian houses if you're traipsing all over the world?"

"I told you I started out that way, McGee. I didn't say I still did that kind of work."

"No, but you sure led me to believe you were operating on a shoestring. When, in fact, you've got yourself quite a worldwide enterprise. You must gross more in a year than I make in ten!"

She was out of the bed, standing toe to toe with him, her head tilted up to meet his challenging gaze. "Is that what all this is about? Can't your almighty male ego accept the idea that a woman might earn more than the great Dan McGee?"

"That's a ridiculous accusation and you know it!" he roared with a sudden and violent indignation. "I'm talking about the fact that you've only been feeding me bits and pieces of your life from the beginning and I want to know why."

"It didn't seem important."

Dan groaned in frustration, damning himself for wanting to believe her. But something wasn't ringing true here and he couldn't put a finger on it. He didn't think she was exactly lying, but she sure wasn't laying all her cards on the table.

"Is the amnesia real?" he asked suddenly.

Jenny looked as if she'd been struck in the face. "Of course."

He eyed her carefully, deciding this much, at least, was true. He sighed, lowering his voice to a gentler, more persuasive tone.

"Then has it occurred to you that we may be involved in something bigger than you and I can handle alone? You haven't exactly been building summer homes in peaceful resort areas, you know." He couldn't help the trace of sarcasm that crept into his tone.

A sharp intelligence gleamed in her dark eyes, reminding

Dan once again that she was not as soft and delicate as she appeared at first glance.

"Believe me, Dan, the first time my car was blown up by PLO terrorists, I figured that out." She brushed past him, obviously determined to put this conversation behind them. "Now, if you're finished with the inquisition, I think I'll take my shower and get ready to leave."

Dan didn't make a move to stop her. Instead, he spun on his heel and marched over to yank open the drapes, staring out across the awakening city. A peaceful blue sky had replaced the pink and lavender dawn, and bright, yellow shafts of sunlight lit the scene.

A moment later he heard the sound of water running and debated saying the hell with it and going in to reinitiate that kiss of the night before. He didn't want to be experiencing these suspicions; it was too bright and sunny outside to be having such disturbing thoughts. But, damn it, she was lying. Every instinctive bone in his body told him so. And simple denial would not drive the thought away.

"Dan?" Lost in thought he hadn't heard her walk up behind him.

"What?"

"Let's not fight like this."

He sighed, turning slowly, feeling his resolve weakening as he saw her in the pink knit dress. She was so lovely; how could he be thinking such uncomplimentary thoughts? But a Venus's-flytrap was fatally attractive to the fly, too, he reminded himself.

"Why didn't you tell me?"

Her eyes were deep pools of contrition as she moved across the room to him, putting her hand on his arm. "I don't know," she admitted softly. "Honestly, Dan, it just didn't seem important. Lots of architects work out of the country. I'm no different; I simply go where the jobs are."

Her nails were stroking a gentle path up the inside of his arm. You're a real sucker, McGee, he told himself, the image of Max Harte and the deadly but lovely Trish coming to mind. He wanted to fling her hand away, but suddenly lacked the strength.

"Yeah," he muttered, "I know lots of architects who work in Beirut. I hate to let you in on this little secret, sweetheart, but they're blowing up more buildings than they're erecting in that city."

"That was five years ago," she said, her delicate touch creating havoc on the inside of his elbow, "and as far as I know, the bank I designed is still standing."

"And Iran?"

"The Shah commissioned that hospital before he was overthrown. It never even got built, which is just as well; God only knows what the Ayatollah's crew would have done to it."

Her soft brown eyes lingered on his face as she gave him a soothing smile. "Let's not fight. I was simply a single woman with an urge to see the world, able to take jobs in places married people with families didn't want to go. That's all there is to it."

He wanted to believe her. God, how he wanted to. But that inner voice was screaming like a civil defense siren.

"And the demilitarized zone?"

"A new PX for the troops stationed in South Korea," she explained. "It wasn't a very pretty building, but then it isn't a very pretty place . . . Aren't you going to kiss me good morning, McGee?"

Dan tried to remind himself that all this was too coincidental, that pretty girls from cattle ranches in southern Oregon did not end up traipsing all over the world. And if they did, London, Paris, and Rome would be more acceptable than the terrorist hot spots. He knew he'd have to find out more about her life after she had arrived in San Francisco wearing that virginal white wedding dress and seeking excitement. For his own peace of mind Dan had to know that she was telling the truth, that all his years of investigative reporting had only served to make him overly suspicious.

As much as he wanted only to taste the honeyed sweetness of her lips, he muttered a low oath, forcing himself to turn away. He jammed his hands into his back pockets, pacing the floor with pent-up anger as he reminded himself that he was furious with her. She was holding back information about herself that could end up getting her killed. Hell, end up getting them both killed.

"Let's get out of here," he finally said, dismissing the matter by tossing her nightgown into the suitcase and closing it with a violent snap. "I want to get back to San Francisco and check out your office as soon as possible."

"Thank you," she murmured, her tone a little sad. "You forgot your coat," she pointed out softly.

He yanked the forgotten trench coat off the chair, reopening the suitcase to stuff it in, not caring that the cleaners had pressed it back into a somewhat acceptable shape.

"Don't thank me," Dan was unable to resist a little sarcasm, "you're the one who promised me a Pulitzer, remember? That's the only reason I'm still hanging around, despite my better judgment."

As his words hung between them, flat and final, Dan felt like a bastard.

Her shoulders slumped. "Oh. Of course . . . I should have thought of that. How stupid of me."

He knew if there was one thing Jenny Winslow wasn't, it was stupid. Despite all the unanswered questions, that little fact had been loud and clear from the beginning.

Chapter Six

Jenny remained silent as they drove away from the hotel, seemingly disinclined to make small talk and unwilling to discuss anything of substance. Dan had been driving about fifteen minutes when a black sedan following his rental car caught his attention. He turned right at the first corner, not terribly surprised when the other vehicle took the same turn. Three more evasive maneuvers proved without a doubt that they were being tailed.

It suddenly occurred to him that there was a chance he'd been set up. That someone had gotten wind of his investigation and had employed this undeniably attractive woman to keep him busy until they could decide what to do with him. In that respect it had already worked. Wasn't he giving up the story to stay with her until he could be sure Jenny was safe?

That was ridiculous, he argued with himself. She could have died in that accident. Dan didn't want to listen to the little voice that pointed out that she could have been used as well, never expecting to get in over her head when she'd entered into the agreement to distract him.

He patted the pocket of his suit, unable to find his pen. "Look in the glove compartment and see if you can find something to write with," he instructed tersely.

She gave him a slightly puzzled look, but did as he told her. "Okay."

A moment later she looked up at him, the first smile in several minutes hovering about the corner of her lips. "How long have you had this rental car?"

"You know that as well as I do. A couple of days."

"Amazing," she murmured, rooting through the collection of half-empty cigarette packs, discarded candy bar wrappers, and assorted papers. "You're going to make some archaeologist in the twenty-third century absolutely ecstatic."

"Just can the humor and see if you can find a pencil."

Her eyes widened momentarily at his harsh tone, but she began to dig a little deeper. "I found one," she proclaimed, holding it up triumphantly. "But it doesn't have a point."

He reached into the pocket of his slacks. "I've got a pocketknife in here somewhere," he said, pulling out a handful of gum wrappers and a pile of change.

"Here, my hands are smaller; let me." Jenny took over the task, delving her hand deep into his pockets. Dan could feel his thigh warming to her probing touch. "Isn't this a lot more fun than fighting?" she asked, grinning up at him.

"You're incorrigible," he grunted, forcing his body not to respond to her teasing fingers.

"I know." She removed the treacherous hand when she found the pocketknife and sharpened the pencil with a few quick, deft strokes. "Now what?"

"Just keep it ready," he instructed, pulling abruptly into an underground parking garage. Jenny slid across the seat toward him. "And fasten your seat belt!"

"Yes sir, Captain Bligh," she retorted, giving him a snappy salute that should have made him furious, but instead made him smile.

Dan's glance in the rearview mirror showed that the car

was still on their tail. "Hold on," he warned, pushing the accelerator to the floor as he shifted through the gears. He negotiated the car through the tortuous twisting curves of the parking garage, the squeal of the tires echoing so that the sound seemed to reverberate from every wall of the concrete cavern. Steering abruptly to the left, he managed to miss a startled pedestrian who was heading toward a green Volvo.

"In a minute, a black sedan is going to pass us. You'll only have a second to get the license plate number. Think you can do it?"

She grabbed a gum wrapper, holding the point of the pencil against the inner surface. "I'll try."

"Okay . . . Here we go." He pulled between a gray van and a red Blazer, slamming on the brakes to bring the car to a shuddering halt. Blue smoke and the smell of burning rubber filled the air.

"Ready?"

"Ready."

The black car screamed around the corner, heading up the ramp. Dan shot out of the concealing spot, rocketed the car back down the way he'd come, and shot out of the parking garage, crashing through the black-and-white wooden barricade to the wide-mouthed consternation of the attendant.

"That was wonderful!" Her brown eyes lit with excitement. "I'll bet Max Harte couldn't have done it any better."

"A danger freak," he groaned. "Just what I need. Did you get the number?"

"Of course." She waved the candy wrapper as a banner of proof.

At her breathtakingly beautiful smile, all earlier irritation vanished. Dan reached out, ruffling her hair with an easy gesture of familiarity.

"Good job. Ready for a little tour through the wine country?"

"I'm ready for anything," she replied, sitting up a little straighter, her gaze bright with expectation.

"Unfortunately, I believe that," he muttered, his laughing blue eyes belying his censorious tone.

They drove in comfortable silence, their mood altered by the tranquillity of scenery that flowed past the window. The grapevines scattered across the rolling, sunlit countryside had the unreal beauty of a picture postcard and Dan found himself wishing that this was merely a pleasure trip so they could take the time to visit one or two of the wineries.

"I wish we could stop," she murmured, as they drove past a large building that resembled a Spanish mission.

"Me too," he agreed instantly. "We'll have to come back."

"I'd like that." She smiled, looking so lovely in the mellow sunshine that Dan wondered how he could have ever been so angry with her.

After his conversation with Marge, he was not particularly surprised when they reached San Francisco and Jenny directed him to a tall tower in the heart of the city. Dan's relaxed mood vanished when he noticed her tense features.

"What's the matter?"

She shook her head, giving a weary shrug. "Nothing."

Something in her eyes started the suspicion churning inside him once again. He reached out, grasping her wrist as she prepared to leave the car.

"Don't give me that. You were thinking of something just now. What was it?"

She looked down at his hand. "You're hurting me."

Instantly his fingers loosened their hold and Dan felt like groaning as he saw the dark red marks braceleting her tender flesh. "I'm sorry," he apologized, "but you're doing it again. You're holding something back."

"No, I wasn't," she denied instantly. "There was just something about this place that almost triggered my memory."

Dan decided he'd been right to bring Jenny here. The key was probably hidden in her office.

His fingers cupped her chin with a gentle touch as he lifted her gaze to his. "You can trust me, Jenny. I want you to know that."

"I know."

Her sad smile touched something deep within him and Dan longed to put his arms around her and assure her that everything would be fine, that he'd always take care of her.

"Let's go," he said instead, turning away abruptly to open his door. "I'm curious to see how a globe-trotting architect decorates her executive offices."

He heard her muffled sigh, but refused to retract his sarcasm. The only sound in the vast underground garage was from their heels clicking on the cement. As he lightly put his hand on her back, Dan felt her shiver. He knew it was fear, rather than desire, that caused the tremor and he had the disquieting sensation that they were walking into a black pit.

Jenny remained silent in the elevator, her eyes glued to the numbers, and Dan wondered what they'd find when they opened her office door.

Whatever he'd been expecting, it certainly wasn't the young man who jumped up from behind a drafting table and swept Jenny into his arms.

"Jennifer, where have you been?" he asked, finally, putting her an arm's length away. "I've been worried sick about you."

"I've been out of town."

"You didn't have a trip planned." His bright green eyes slid past her to Dan, who was still standing in the open doorway. "Was it business?"

Before Jenny could answer, Dan cut in. "She took a vacation," he said blandly, his gaze daring the man to challenge the statement. "I thought she looked tired and suggested a rest."

The man's judicious gaze swept over Dan before returning to Jenny. "What happened to your head?"

"I had a little accident," she murmured, rubbing the row of stitches.

"Accident? What kind of accident?"

"Nothing important." Dan brushed aside Jenny's flirtation with death with a careless wave of his hand. "She's going to be just fine."

So this was the partner, he mused, taking in the man who wore his European styled navy suit with the air of an individual who'd never worn anything else. The guy had a slim waist, well-defined muscles, a handsome face and—when he'd greeted her—a devastating smile. Standing beside Jenny, with his thick blond hair and healthy tan, they looked like bookends.

Dan shifted his appraising glance to the drafting board the man had abandoned. It figured. Besides, his other attributes, Jenny's partner was disgustingly neat. Dan hated him.

"I didn't catch your name." The young man's tone was just barely civil, and a proprietary arm curved about Jenny's waist.

"That's probably because I didn't throw it."

Their challenging gazes held in the silence that descended. Jenny exhaled a long, exasperated sigh that ruffled her bangs.

"For heaven's sake," she muttered, "Dan McGee, this is Lance Griffen, my partner. Lance, Dan's a friend of mine."

Lance arched a blond brow. "I've never heard you mention him."

"Don't feel bad, Griffen," Dan said, "Jenny and I don't spend our time talking about you, either." He scored a direct hit; Lance's face darkened with a bright red flush that rose from his starched white collar.

"Jenny?" Lance questioned the unfamiliar name. He seemed to be on the verge of saying something, then changed his mind. "Well, next time you take off, Jennifer, I'd suggest you leave a number. This place has been a madhouse the past two days."

"I thought you told me you were all caught up, darling," Dan drawled. Jenny glared in response to the endearment.

"There are two guys who've been back five times in the past two days," Lance continued.

"Who are they?" she asked. Dan felt like applauding her performance as she kept her tone studiously casual. Only the slight shadow that moved across her eyes revealed her distress.

Lance shrugged. "They wouldn't leave a card."

"What did they want?" This from Dan.

The younger man leaned against the desk, folding his arms over his pin-striped vest. "Since this is an architectural office, I can only surmise they're in the market for an architect." His smooth brow furrowed in absent thought. "Although, to tell you the truth, Jennifer, neither of them looks like your usual clientele."

"What do you mean?" she asked, exchanging a quick glance with Dan. He nodded, letting her know she was doing fine.

"One guy looks like he works out, but he's almost too slick, if you know what I mean. He made my skin crawl. The guy with him looks like a walking soda machine and I swear, his suit is ten years old if it's a day. You'd never believe the fit." His gaze moved to Dan. "Or maybe you would," he amended dryly.

Dan almost hoped that Lance Griffen had something to do with Jenny's dilemma. He'd love an excuse to break the kid's handsome face.

"Lance," Jenny suggested softly, watching the thundercloud move across Dan's face, "it's past lunchtime. Have you eaten?"

"No, I was too busy trying to field your calls. I've been stalling, telling everyone you're out inspecting a job, but I can't keep that up."

She smiled, patting his cheek. "Why don't you go to lunch and I'll just turn things over to the answering service."

"You're not here to work?"

"I'm picking up some blueprints for Mr. McGee," she lied adroitly. "Then we're driving out to Napa Valley to look at his land."

"I don't remember seeing any blueprints for a McGee," he argued. "What is it?"

"A winery," Dan answered.

"An inn," Jenny replied at the same time.

Lance's face mirrored his confusion. "Well, which is it? A winery or an inn?"

"It's a winery with an inn on the property." Jenny once again proved her unnerving ability for prevarication. "It should prove popular with the tourists, don't you think?"

Dan watched Jenny's partner digest that information. "It just might work," he agreed. "But I still don't remember seeing anything like that around here."

"I've been working on it at home."

"Oh." His expression remained puzzled.

Dan moved to Jenny's side, looping his arm over her shoulders as he gazed down into her face with an adoring, sensual smile. "I insisted Jenny work on this project personally," he stated blithely, "since she knows exactly what I like. Don't you sweetheart?" He pressed a kiss against her temple.

Jenny drilled her high heel down on his foot. "Oh, excuse me, darling!" Her voice dripped with syrup as Dan sucked in a harsh breath. "That was incredibly clumsy of me."

Dan managed a valiant smile as he squeezed her shoulders with a casual-looking but unnecessary force. "Don't worry about it; I know what an endearing klutz you can be from time to time. That's one of the things I love about you."

Obviously Lance had witnessed all the lovey-dovey stuff he was prepared to take. "I think I'll go to lunch."

"That's a wonderful idea." Jenny's face was wreathed in a breathtaking smile as she reached behind Dan's back, taking hold of his waist and twisting it between her fingers.

"Take your time," Dan advised, his own broad grin not displaying his pain as his hand dropped down to pinch her bottom.

"Oh!"

"What did you say?" Lance turned in the doorway, eyeing them both curiously over his shoulder.

"I didn't say a thing," Dan said truthfully.

"Neither did I," Jenny alleged.

He rubbed his square, handsome jaw. "Are you sure?"

"Positive."

"Absolutely."

"That's the second time, I've thought I heard voices," he muttered, "I must be working too hard."

"Wait a minute!" Dan's harsh tone caught and held their attention. "What do you mean?"

Lance shrugged. "I dropped in here last night to pick up some specs I'd forgotten and thought I heard someone talking. But when I opened the door, no one was here."

"Are you sure?"

"Well, I didn't search the place, if that's what you mean. But the lights were off, and the place was as quiet as a tomb."

"What did you do then?"

"Why?" His green eyes held a definite hint of suspicion.

"Don't mind Dan," Jenny broke in with another quick lie. "His hobby is parapsychology. He's so eager to find himself a ghost, his imagination sometimes takes right off."

"Weird," Lance muttered, leaving the office and closing the door behind him. Dan pressed his fingers against her lips and they both remained silent until they heard the elevator begin its descent.

Jenny spun on him. "You pinched me!"

"You ground your damn high heel into my foot first, sweetheart," he reminded her.

"That's because you let Lance think there was something going on between us."

"There is," he countered swiftly. "I'm trying to save your fool neck. Or have you forgotten how you got that needlework on your forehead?"

"Of course I haven't forgotten. But that's no reason to let him think we were off somewhere sleeping together."

"We were."

"You know very well what I mean." Her dark eyes flashed at him.

"Of course I do. And so does he, which is exactly how I want it. The guy's in love with you, Jenny. It's just as well he understands he doesn't have a chance."

Her mouth dropped open as she stared at him. "*In love?*

McGee, of all your ideas, that's just about the dumbest yet. Lance and I work together, period."

His fingers curved around her shoulders and Dan had the sudden urge to shake her until her lovely white teeth rattled.

"Maybe that's the way you see it, but the kid's got an entirely different idea about your future together. How old is he, anyway? Aren't you robbing the cradle?"

"He's twenty six," she retorted, "Only four years younger than me. If I wanted to have an affair with Lance Griffen—which I certainly don't—let me point out that you men have always played around with younger women. How about that old adage about sauce for the goose being sauce for the gander?"

"You've got it wrong, for one thing. The male is the gander. So you should be saying what's sauce for the gander is sauce for the goose."

She tossed her head. "I know which is which. Don't forget, I grew up around animals. It just sounds better the other way." Comprehension slowly dawned and her eyes widened. "Are you jealous?"

Dan's palms shaped her shoulders in a soft, caressing gesture. "Of course I am."

"Oh." She fell silent, studying the blue carpet underfoot with feigned interest.

"Oh," he mimicked lightly. "Is that all you have to say?"

She slowly, solemnly lifted her head. "No. Because I hate every woman you've ever known, McGee."

He had heard an amazing series of lies fall trippingly off Jenny's tongue, but from the glow in her dark eyes, Dan didn't think she was lying about this.

"We'll have to discuss this in depth later," he suggested, his thumbs stroking the soft skin of her throat.

"Later," she agreed softly.

"I suppose we'd better go through these files before your partner comes back," he suggested, his tone displaying the fact that it was not his first choice.

She giggled, going up on her toes to press a light kiss against his lips. "Lance will probably take a very long lunch," she predicted. "Since I think you scared him away."

The fleeting warmth was gone from his lips much too soon as she slipped out of his arms and began pulling open file drawers.

"Well, at least I accomplished something today," Dan muttered.

They sifted through the files carefully, Jenny rifling each set of papers, her expression changing from hopeful to depressed by the time they'd reached the end of the alphabet.

"I'm sorry," she said, slumping into a chair. "But nothing rings a bell."

Dan felt as disappointed as Jenny looked, but decided this was no time to put additional pressure on her. "That's okay. It was just an idea."

She propped her elbows onto the desk, bracing her chin with her hands. "Now what?"

What the hell would Max Harte do now? Dan asked himself. "We'll try your place. Since you didn't let your partner in on this, maybe you've stashed something over there."

She eyed him with interest. "What makes you think I didn't tell Lance anything?"

"That much was obvious since the guy didn't even know where you went. And I didn't exactly see you jumping in to volunteer any information earlier. Whatever you were up to, Jenny, you were acting on your own."

"You don't think he has anything to do with all this, do you?"

"Do you?"

She sighed. "I don't want to. But you're right, I don't trust anyone right now." Her expression softened. "Correction, I don't trust anyone but you." Dan regretted ever harboring an ounce of suspicion toward Jenny Winslow as her eyes brightened with unshed tears.

"That's a start," he said gruffly. "Ready to try your place?"

She blinked away the tears as she rose from the chair with a slow, weary motion. "Might as well," she agreed without enthusiasm.

Jenny didn't object to Dan's arm around her as the elevator took them back down to the parking garage. When they got there, Dan caught a familiar sight out of the corner of his eye.

"Stay right here," he instructed, putting her behind a broad, concrete pillar. Her dark eyes displayed confusion, but she nodded.

Dan watched the two men making their way toward the elevator. They were definitely not the ones Lance had described, but he recognized them all the same. They were the same two men he'd seen entering the hotel from the parking lot the day before in Sacramento. The two dark-suited men he'd idly wondered about. And, unless he was way off base, they were the two guys in the black sedan.

Dan made his way stealthily around a row of parked cars, watching as the men stepped into the elevator. Entering the adjoining one, he forced himself to count to ten before pushing the number of Jenny's floor. But he hadn't waited long enough. When the door opened, he glanced out, not at all surprised to see them headed down the hallway toward her office.

The sound of the elevator gave him away and one of the men turned, spotting him. "Hey!"

Instantly deciding that even Max Harte would opt for an

honorable retreat about now, Dan punched the button, shutting the door in their faces as he sent the car back to the garage.

"Come on," he grabbed Jenny's arm, yanking her in the direction of the parked rental car.

She had to run to keep up with him. "Dan, what in the world is going on?"

"Be quiet," he instructed, his mind whirling as he attempted to figure a way out of this. Just in time, the answer arrived in the form of Lance, who drove into the garage.

"We're borrowing your car." Dan yanked open the door of the Corvette and jerked the young man from the driver's seat.

"What the hell?"

"Don't ask questions, Lance," Jenny advised, sliding into the passenger seat. "I promise it's only for a little while. Take some cab fare out of petty cash."

Before Lance could argue, Dan had fit his bulk into the bucket seat and they were headed up the ramp to the street.

"Now that we've stolen my partner's car, do you think you could tell me what's going on?" Jenny asked with amazing calm.

"In a minute." Dan tossed a twenty dollar bill at the parking lot attendant. "Keep the change," he advised, rewarded as the gate instantly rose.

Directly outside the garage, he pulled over to the curb. "It's those two we lost in Sacramento," he explained. "Since they're not looking for this car, I think it'll be safe to park here and see if you recognize them."

"I'll try."

He managed a tight smile. "Good girl."

She bristled instinctively. "I'm not a girl!"

This time Dan's smile was a little warmer. "I know. I just

don't think this is the time to get into your more womanly attributes, okay?" His gaze moved over her body with unmistakable insinuation.

"That's better," she murmured, directing her attention back to the street.

A moment later, as predicted, the black car came barreling by. Since the garage was located on a dead-end street, the driver had to drive past Dan and Jenny. Dan scrunched down, trying to be as inconspicuous as a six-foot-four-inch man could manage in the front seat of a bright red Corvette.

"Well?"

"I've never seen them before in my life."

"Are you sure?"

She lifted her hands in a helpless gesture. "Not that I can remember . . . But that doesn't help a whole lot, does it?"

Not much, he agreed mentally. "Don't worry," he said aloud. "At least we've got their license number. I'll get on that as soon as we get to the hotel."

"Hotel?"

"You don't think I'm taking you back to your apartment now, do you?"

She thought about that for a long, silent moment. "I suppose that's not such a good idea," she finally agreed. "But what if the answer is there, Dan?"

"We'll get you settled in and I'll go check out your place."

"But, if those men show up . . ."

She reached across the cockpitlike interior of the car, pressing her palm against his chest, her voice vibrating with honest emotion.

"If you got hurt, Dan, I don't know what I'd do."

He felt as if her soft touch was burning his skin right through the material of his shirt and vowed that whatever was going on, he was going to get it settled once and for all.

Then he and Jenny Winslow could get down to more important business.

"Please don't go. This is getting far too dangerous."

"Hell, honey, it was already too dangerous when you got on that plane the other night," he pointed out with a terrible foreboding that it could get even worse.

Chapter Seven

As Dan pulled the car under the large white awning that extended over the drive of the hotel, Jenny's eyes widened. "The Fairmont?"

"Do you have any objections?"

"Not really, but I expected something a little less . . ." Her voice dropped off as she searched for an appropriate word.

"Expensive?"

"That's it," she admitted.

"Hey, don't sweat the small stuff. Fortunately, *Newsview*'s expense account is extremely generous. Especially when I'm tracking down a Pulitzer."

"Wait just a minute!" She put her hand on his arm as he prepared to get out of the car. "Dan, we agreed that I'd pay you back for my half of all this as soon as you get my checkbook from my town house."

Refusing to listen to a word of protest, he bent down, giving her a quick kiss. "Hey, even in these days of liberated females, when a man takes his lady to a hotel, he pays the bill." With a wide smile, he unfolded his tall frame from the car.

Before Jenny could answer, a liveried doorman, clad in a black uniform with broad red epaulets and shiny brass buttons, opened the passenger door and Jenny had no choice but to follow Dan into the hotel.

"McGee, we have to have a serious talk."

"I agree," he surprised her by saying. "And we will, as soon as we get upstairs to the privacy of our own room." Dan did not see anyone suspicious as they made their way across the richly decorated lobby with marble pillars and a gilt-framed ceiling that recalled San Francisco's golden era.

He had no idea whether or not *Newsview* would balk at the bill for the Nob Hill hotel, but to Dan the hotel had always echoed the very essence of the city—cosmopolitan, sophisticated, and romantic. Since discovering those identical qualities in Jenny, the Fairmont had seemed the only logical place to stay, and if *Newsview* didn't like it, he'd spring for the bill himself. It would be worth it.

Jenny didn't utter a word when he registered them as Mr. and Mrs. Daniel McGee. In fact, she didn't say anything as they were led to their room.

"Nice view," Dan decreed, tossing his jacket onto a chair and moving across the plush carpeting to look out at the cobalt waters of San Francisco bay.

"I've seen Alcatraz."

A slight irritation tinged her words and Dan put his arm around her shoulders in a casual gesture. "Hungry?"

"No." She shrugged off his arm, wrapping her own about herself as she moved away from him, her gaze still directed out the window.

Dan wondered if anything about Jenny Winslow was going to turn out to be simple. Here he was, in one of the most romantic hotels in the world, and the lady had just encased herself in enough ice to create a new continent. He threw himself onto the bed, putting his arms under his head as he watched her reach into his jacket pocket and pull out his crumpled pack of cigarettes on the first try. His lighter took a little more searching and he could feel Jenny's irritation mounting as she extracted various items before locating it.

As she lit the cigarette, Dan remembered that the only other time he'd seen her smoke was on the plane that first evening. Obviously, the lady was not thrilled with their situation.

"The beds are comfortable," he offered, trying to find something she'd like. "Real down pillows."

"Down pillows make me sneeze."

"Oh."

Silence settled around them, thick and stifling, like early morning fog. Muffling a deep sigh of frustration, Dan rose, going over to the table where she'd placed the cigarettes.

"Are you going to sulk all day or tell me what's bugging you?" he asked calmly, lighting one of his own.

She turned on him, her dark eyes flashing. "Look, McGee, I'll admit I needed some help and you looked like a man I could trust, but I didn't invite you to march into my life like some damned storm trooper and take it over! This is my problem, and I'd appreciate it if you'd just let me handle it my own way!" She glared at him, then spun around to stare out across the bay.

Dan remained silent as Jenny puffed furiously on the cigarette waiting to see if she had anything more to add. It had bothered him from the beginning that she was taking it all so calmly, although he'd attributed that to her poise and self-control. It wasn't surprising that she'd begin to react, nor was he particularly disturbed that she was taking her stress out on him.

"I don't have any money or clothes. I'm totally dependent on you, which undoubtedly strokes that excessive male ego to Olympian heights. You've probably run off my partner for good, and so far you've spent more time spying on me than you have trying to figure out who's chasing me. You've told practically the entire world I'm your wife and you've moved me from hotel room to hotel room like I'm just another suitcase."

She took a deep breath before continuing. "You've infiltrated yourself into the most personal aspects of my life— buying my underwear, for Pete's sake—and you managed to drag out a story about my family that I've never told anyone. You're driving me crazy, McGee, so knock it off!"

Jenny turned to grind the cigarette out with unnecessary force, her eyes gleaming with unshed tears. Dan didn't respond immediately, giving her time to recover her composure.

"Is that all?" he asked finally. "Nothing about squeezing the toothpaste in the middle of the tube or leaving wet towels on the bathroom floor?"

"Believe it or not," she said in a somewhat shaky voice, "I'm an extremely competent woman. In fact, I've run off more than one man because I'm not willing to give up my hard won independence."

"I believe that," he replied simply.

"But this—this problem has created such an aberrant situation, I'm behaving totally out of character."

He nodded, his expression grave. "I also believe that."

"What you're seeing is not the real Jennifer Winslow," she insisted.

Dan put out his own cigarette, finally moving to within inches of her. "I can't accept that," he argued.

"You have to."

"No."

"It's a fact. Even the famous Dan McGee can't argue with the truth."

"That's where you're wrong, sweetheart. I have a funny

habit of never taking anything at face value. You're not being completely honest with me."

"Now we're back to that again. My foreign work," she snapped, tilting back her head to meet his challenging gaze head on.

Dan shook his head. "That's not what I'm talking about. I'm talking about the other side of Jennifer Winslow."

"What other side?"

A slow smile curved his lips. "You're two women, sweetheart, and while I admire the stubborn, pragmatic lady architect who knows exactly what she wants out of life, the lady I'm about to kiss is human enough to accept a little assistance from time to time when things get out of hand. She's also the one who knows when to stop thinking and let herself experience some honest emotions."

Jenny backed away, holding out her hands to ward off his huskily stated intention. "Good try, but that polished little line isn't going to work."

"It isn't a line," he murmured, moving unhesitatingly toward her.

"It still isn't going to work."

He arched a black brow. "Isn't it?"

She backed up two more steps. "No. In fact, I think it's time for me to leave and settle this problem by myself."

He spanned the gap between them in one long stride. "You know I'm not going to let you do that, Jenny. For your own good."

The backs of her legs were against the mattress, blocking any further retreat. Dan reached out to take her hands, but she suddenly scrambled up and over the mattress, her brown eyes revealing her distress as they flew about the room, seeking any means of escape.

"You can't keep me a prisoner in here, Dan."

He noted with some degree of satisfaction that each backward step only took her further away from the door. He hoped Jenny wouldn't try to make a break for it. It was difficult to remember how delicate she was and he was afraid if he had to tackle her, she would only end up with more bruises.

"I can and I will, if necessary," he countered. "For your own good."

"I'm sick and tired of you telling me what to do! I want to make my own decisions for a change."

"Fine."

Her eyes displayed a certain wariness, but at least she stayed where she was, Dan noticed, feeling her vacillation.

"What do you mean by that?"

"Kiss me and tell me you still want to leave."

"That's ridiculous," she spat out.

He folded his arms over his chest. "Scared?"

"Of course not. It just wouldn't prove anything."

"Yes, it would."

"You're that sure of your masculine appeal?"

"I'm that sure of *us*," he countered.

She shook her head, eyeing him with a mixture of admiration and frustration. "Your ego, McGee, is not to be believed."

He smiled. "You just don't want to admit what we've got going for ourselves here, because you can't imagine yourself getting involved with a rumpled, jaded old journalist."

"You're not old," she answered automatically. "And any man who would go out and buy a woman he'd just met a romantic pink dress is far from jaded."

Dan tried not to be distracted by the fact that she hadn't denied the rumpled part of his description. Oh well, he decided pragmatically, two out of three . . .

"Kiss me, Jenny." He held out his arms invitingly.

"No way."

"Kiss me and if you don't want to stay I'll give you cab fare home and move out of your way."

His words were a deep velvet invitation and Dan hoped this risk wouldn't backfire on him. He wasn't about to let her out of the room, no matter what he'd just promised. If she still insisted, he'd have to destroy whatever measure of trust he'd established thus far in their relationship.

"*Lend* me the cab fare," she corrected firmly. "I intend to pay back every penny you've spent on me so far."

"Lend," he agreed.

"One kiss? That's all?"

Dan forced his voice into a casual tone he was far from feeling. "One kiss."

He watched as she chewed thoughtfully on her thumbnail, eyeing him with an expression reminiscent of a small animal cornered by a snake.

"And then I can leave?"

"If you still want to."

Her gaze narrowed. "I can't believe even you feel confident enough to think you can change my mind with a single kiss."

His answering gaze was solemn, his words spoken with a vibrating intensity. "I'm hoping I can." That much was definitely true.

"All right," she decided. "One kiss."

"Come here." His husky voice betrayed the desire he'd kept safely restrained.

Jenny shook her head, silently refusing his murmured request.

"Sweetheart, there's a queen-sized mattress between us," he pointed out.

"I only agreed to a kiss, Dan, not a wrestling match."

He wanted to strangle her even as he found himself reluctantly admiring her ploy. Not that it would work, of course. But it was a nice try.

"Didn't anyone ever tell you that you can get yourself in a lot of trouble dangling a challenge in front of a man who thrives on doing the impossible?"

Before she could answer, Dan was over the bed, his broad hand on her neck, his fingers splayed on the back of her head. As his head slowly descended, Jenny shut her eyes, waiting for the kiss that Dan had no intention of rushing.

"What do you think you're doing?"

Her lashes flew open as he buried his face in her hair, inhaling the rich scent and savoring the feel of it against his cheek while imagining how it was going to feel spread across his chest after making love.

"Preliminaries," he murmured, pressing his lips against her temple.

"That's not fair," she protested, even as her hands moved up his arms to his shoulders. "You're cheating." Her breath caught momentarily in her throat as Dan's lips trailed a path around the back of her ear.

"So are you," he argued, his tongue flicking out to briefly explore the soft convolutions. "You're cheating with this evocative feminine scent that surrounds you like a perfumed mist; you're cheating by looking more enticing with every passing moment."

He closed his teeth, tugging lightly on the delicate skin of her earlobe in a seductive manner that made her gasp.

"And you're cheating by tasting so damn good." He felt her shudder as he slowly trailed his lips along her jawline, his breath fanning her flushed skin. When his mouth finally covered hers, their breath mingled as they sighed their pleasure in unison.

As his mouth moved on hers, first softly, then with

increasing strength, Jenny leaned into his arms, suc-
cumbing to his steady pressure as he urged her against his
thighs. Dan's pulse pounded as her body molded itself
against his frame, and he moved his hand up her side to cup
the tender fullness of her breast.

Jenny moaned, but Dan's mouth swallowed the soft
sound. He parted his lips, inviting her tongue, and she
complied, first with an endearing hesitancy, then growing
bolder as her own previously banked fires of desire began to
flare.

Dan's head swam as her tongue swept the dark interior of
his mouth, like fingers of flame against his sensitized skin.
His hand moved down her side, over her hip, caressing her
womanly curves with a restraint that he would have never
believed possible.

"Sweet Jenny," he murmured, "you feel so good." He
lowered his lips to the thrusting fullness of her breasts, his
breath wafting through the knit fiber to heat the skin underneath.

"But I need to feel more of you, sweetheart." He reached
down, gathering the hem of the garment in his fingers as he
slowly lifted it up her thighs.

"Dan . . ."

His mind burned with his body's need and Dan told himself that her ragged little cry was not really a refusal. "Shh,"
he whispered against her lips. "It'll be okay, Jenny. Trust
me."

His mouth pressed against hers with renewed force as he
brought the dress past her hips, over her stomach, and up
her rib cage, exposing the swollen flesh of her breasts as
they pressed against the diaphanous fabric of the rose
teddy.

"Lift your arms for me darlin'," he instructed, his lips
plucking enticingly at hers, inviting acquiescence.

Jenny did as requested, her body trembling even as a slight, regretful sigh escaped her lips. Unable to give her time to change her mind, Dan pulled her down onto the bed, forcing himself not to shred the silky material denying him access to her gleaming skin. Patience had never been one of Dan McGee's strongest attributes, but he wanted to please Jenny, to make her happy, to draw out every sensation to its fullest rather than take her in the whirlwind his body was demanding.

He cupped her breast with his wide palm, rewarded as she arched her back off the mattress to press herself against his touch. He pushed aside the rose lace, his fingers capturing her dark pink nipple. As he lightly tugged at it, Jenny flinched, then relaxed, murmuring soft sounds of pleasure.

"Do you like that?" he asked, his thumb and forefinger teasing at the thrusting bud. "Do you like the feel of my hands on you as much as I enjoy touching you?"

She writhed under his touch as he turned his attention to her other breast while his tongue swathed a fiery path between them, down her shimmering body. The teddy fell away, drifting to the floor in a satin puddle.

"Do you have to ask? My God, Dan, surely you can see what you're doing to me."

"I need to hear you say it," he replied, his lips plucking at the soft skin of her abdomen. "I want to know I can bring you pleasure, Jenny."

"Yes," she admitted on a ragged gasp as his tongue traced damp trails along her satiny skin. "I love the feel of your hands on me."

"Good." His hands moved to cup the soft flesh of her buttocks, lifting her toward him as his teeth nibbled teasingly at the inside of her thighs.

"Admit you want to stay with me," he demanded, his fingers teasing the soft flesh hidden within the dark honey curls.

His reckless insistence reminded Jenny of their earlier argument. "Dan, don't. You can't, please—" She struggled for words as her hands pressed against his shoulders.

"Jenny, we've been heading toward this since that first moment in the airport." He shifted his body, pressing it over hers, boldly inserting his leg between her creamy thighs.

"It's too soon," she protested weakly. Dan knew it was impossible for her to ignore the hard evidence of his desire and from her soft moan as she moved underneath him, he knew that he was not alone in his need.

"It's not too soon," he argued, his fingers trailing up her inner thigh in feathery, tantalizing strokes. She twisted her head into the soft down pillow as he reached his seductive quest. Oh, God, Dan agonized, as he found her warm and welcoming, she was driving him crazy.

"I want you so badly, Jenny. And you want me too. You can't deny that." As Dan deepened his seductively probing touch, Jenny cried out, her body responding of its own volition to the intimacy of his embrace, even as she sought to end it.

"I can't deny it, Dan. But you want more than I can give."

"I want you." His hands, his lips, his body, all pressed his case with a seductiveness that increased the level of Dan's own desire.

"You want all of me," she argued.

His lips had tasted the soft skin at her ankle, his teeth had nibbled at the back of her knees, and now he was kissing the skin of her inner thigh, but at her ragged accusation he raised his head, his heated gaze colliding with hers.

"Would that be so terrible?"

"I think so."

"Why?"

He didn't want to be having this conversation. Even now he could feel Jenny garnering strength, gathering up the scattered vestiges of her self-restraint. He shifted his body in order to reestablish superiority. She was so little, so delicate.

Dan knew that, although he might technically be accused of using force in the beginning, Jenny wanted this as much as he did. The way she trembled at his touch demonstrated that. Her body was warm and willing, even if her mind had not been able to breach that final barrier.

"I'm afraid," she admitted in a whisper.

Dan chose to misunderstand. He pushed the love-tumbled hair back from her face, kissing her frowning lips. "I know, sweetheart. But I promise, I'll take care of you."

She grasped a handful of his jet curls, lifting his head with a force that surprised him. "Don't play games with me, McGee," she instructed firmly. "You know very well what I mean. I'm afraid of *you*."

He pretended wounded outrage. "Me? Jenny, I'd never hurt you."

Her brown eyes were solemn, sparked with that intelligence that he found so inexplicably sensual. "You could," she corrected. "I've already lowered my barriers and let my vulnerability show. I turn to putty every time you touch me; I've told you all about my family, my need for success. My God, I've given you a road map of all my weak points." Her tone was filled with regret and self-directed anger.

Dan heaved a long, frustrated sigh, lifting himself off her body to a sitting position on the edge of the bed. "Doesn't that prove something important, Jenny? That I know all those little clues about you and haven't used them against you?"

She sat up herself, pulling her knees up against her

breasts and wrapping her hands about her legs as if to shield herself from his warm gaze. Dan reached down, plucking the teddy from the floor.

"Here."

"Thank you." She looked up at him. "I don't suppose you'd want to turn around for a minute?"

Dan thought it was a little late to be displaying signs of feminine modesty, since he'd already seen every inch of her lush body. If he lived a hundred years, he decided, he'd never understand the female of the species. Muttering a low oath, he obliged her by directing his gaze out the window.

The bay was filled with recreational sailors, sails fluttering in the wind in a way that made Dan wish fervently that he'd met Jenny Winslow in any other way. How he'd love to be down there with her now, sharing a chilled bottle of champagne, the sunlit afternoon, and the fresh sea breeze. The idea made him smile.

"I'm glad you find all this so damn funny." Her voice held that hard edge he'd heard when she'd talked about her parents.

"I was thinking about sailing," he responded noncommittally. "Do you like to sail?"

"I love it," she admitted. "I haven't had much time for it the past few years, though."

"Too busy working?"

"Uh-huh."

"Me too."

There was a long, significant silence as they both stared out the window. Then Jenny reached out, putting her hand on his arm in what he took as a conciliatory gesture.

"Dan?"

"Yeah?" While no longer angry, he had no intention of looking like a pushover in the hands of a beautiful woman.

"If we get out of this, do you think you could take a little time off and go sailing with me?"

He felt as if she'd just lifted ten tons and a hundred years from his shoulders. "*When* we get out of all this, we'll take a lot of time off and do everything we've been wanting to do," he agreed.

He leered in an unthreatening way. "In fact, if you want, I'll turn in my resignation and we can begin playing right now."

She laughed softly, shaking her head. "You know the problem with you, McGee, I never know when to take you seriously."

At this point Dan didn't know himself how many of these promises were uttered as automatic seduction ploys and how many he really meant. He did know one thing, though— despite the danger, he was in no hurry to end this forced alliance.

They fell silent again as he rose from the bed. When he asked for the spare key to her town house she'd picked up at the office, Jenny was hesitant.

"I worry about you going over there alone, Dan."

He shrugged, a feigned, casual gesture he thought Max might use about now. "Hey, wouldn't you like some of your own clothes? Besides, there's a distinct possibility the solution to all this might be in your files at home."

She sighed, admitting his reasoning, but obviously disliking the idea. "I don't want you to get hurt."

"I won't."

Her smile wavered a bit as she looked up at him. "Promise?"

Dan allowed himself the pleasure of one more kiss, the brief flare causing fireworks to go off behind his eyes.

"Sweetheart, when you look at me with those velvety brown eyes, I'd promise you anything."

She was obviously trying to look stern, but the lambent glow in her eyes gave her away. "Don't you take anything seriously?" she asked softly.

Dan's answering smile didn't quite meet his eyes. "Of course I do. In fact, when I get back, I'd say we're long overdue for a talk about that particular subject."

"Oh, oh," she attempted a joking demeanor, but as their gaze held neither one was laughing. "If I were as intelligent as I like to believe, I should probably run away as soon as you go through that door."

"It wouldn't work," he said, once again experiencing the sensation of drowning as he looked deep into her eyes. "Because I'd find you, Jenny Winslow. If I had to devote the rest of my life to the quest."

Even as he heard himself saying the words, Dan knew they were true. My God, he thought, what had this woman *done* to him?

"You're a stubborn man, Dan McGee," she whispered, her hand trembling as she reached out to lightly stroke his cheek. Once again the silken web of desire was settling over them, but this time Dan was strong enough to keep his mind on the task at hand.

"Incredibly," he agreed cheerfully, turning his head to press a quick, hard kiss against the skin of her palm. "But so are you. That's what's making this little contest so intriguing."

"Contest?" A little smile hovered at the corners of her lips as he stood up, grinning down at her.

"Contest. We both know we're going to end up making love, Jenny. The question is, which of us is going to be the one to precipitate the event? I'm used to calling the shots and every indication you've given me so far indicates you're a lady used to getting her own way. If either of us had a lick of sense we'd quit playing these games and give in to what is bound to be an unforgettable experience."

"You're too perceptive, McGee. In fact, I'm beginning to understand how you get your interview subjects to crack," Jenny commented with a sudden note of seriousness. "You just keep hammering away, hitting nearer and nearer the truth until finally you've gotten exactly what you're after."

"There's nothing wrong with that. After all, Jenny, every-thing I've done so far has been—"

"For my own good," she muttered sulkily. "I've certainly heard that before." Then her expression changed. "Dan," she whispered shakily, "please be careful."

She rose gracefully from the bed, going up on her toes to give him a long, lingering kiss that threatened to destroy the intention he had of getting out of there without ravish-ing Jenny Winslow in every conceivable way—and a few inconceivable ones, too.

Forcing himself to release her slender body that felt so right in his arms, he backed away, grabbed his jacket from the chair, and stuck her keys into a pocket.

"When I get back," he said, turning in the doorway, "we're going to have that talk."

Jenny nodded, her eyes wide and solemn as she watched him leave.

"Fasten the chain on this door," he instructed on a gritty tone that was meant to disguise how desperately he wanted to protect her from any harm.

"I was going to do that," she said, a flare of temper bringing color back into her cheeks.

"That's my girl," he murmured, throwing her a kiss as he left the room. He waited outside the door until he heard the chain slide into place. Then, sticking his hands deep into his pockets, he headed toward the elevator.

All he had to do was let himself into her apartment,

gather up her files and some clothes, and bring them back to the hotel. It should be a piece of cake. It should be. If he could avoid two guys driving around in a black sedan and another pair of thugs who shouldn't be that difficult to spot. In a city known for elegant attire, another suit as old as his should stand out like a blizzard in July.

Chapter Eight

Dan located Jenny's restored Victorian town house without difficulty. Not wanting to tip his hand in case her pursuers happened to drive by, he parked the car in front of a bright blue house three doors down the street. Then, congratulating himself as he pulled her key out of his pocket on the first try, he climbed the wooden steps to her front door.

Dan cursed under his breath when he discovered it was unlocked. For an intelligent woman, she sure as hell could act like a bloody fool, he thought as he entered the narrow, darkly lit foyer. A silent warning bell tolled in his head the moment before he reached the small, boxlike room that had once served as a parlor.

Of course it was unlocked—someone had been here before him. Everything about Jenny Winslow demonstrated she was a paragon of efficiency. He'd expected her home to make a nun's cell look disorganized, but this place looked as if it had had its own private earthquake, followed by several gale force hurricanes. As his eyes roamed the vandalism, the short hairs suddenly stood up on the back of his neck.

"Don't make a move, unless you want it to be your last." The gruff voice issued the warning as a gun was pressed into his back.

Dan closed his eyes for a long moment, reminding himself that he'd been in sticky situations before. All he had to do was keep his head and he could probably talk his way out of this one.

"If you're here to rob the place, don't let me interrupt," he said. "We've all got to make a living, right?"

"If there's one thing I hate, it's a joker."

Dan's heart sank as a second voice, laced with a decidedly foreign accent, joined the first.

"How come you guys had to tear the place apart like this? Couldn't you have left it nice and tidy like the office?"

"How the hell did you—" The first man's question was cut off by the second, whom Dan realized was in charge of this particular scavenger hunt.

"That's a very clever deduction. Now why don't you continue to demonstrate your intelligence by giving us the film and forget you ever met Jennifer Winslow?"

Forget Jenny? They may as well try to rid the city of fog, or stop the sun from rising over the hills and sinking into the bay each night. Everything about Jenny Winslow was engraved into his memory and nothing these two thugs could do would ever change that fact.

"Film?" Dan wished he knew what was going on. Maybe, if he kept them talking, they'd let slip what it was that Jenny had been so eager to keep from them.

"Let me just waste the guy and get it over with." Dan felt the barrel of the gun pressing a little deeper in his back. His mind scrambled to come up with a stalling tactic.

"If you do that, you'll never find out where the film is," he replied in a remarkably calm voice. Dan wondered idly if he might have a career as an actor when all this was over. It was only a bluff, but from the looks of this place, they still hadn't located whatever film they'd been seeking.

"We can always drag it out of the girl," the second man reminded him in an accent that was vaguely English, but not quite. "In fact, I'd rather do it that way; it could make for quite a stimulating afternoon, watching that cool bird crack."

As the man moved out of the shadows, Dan was able to see his adversary and knew these had to be the guys Lance described. He had the body of a weightlifter and, though he was a bit short, what he lacked in height he made up for in physical strength. As Dan's eyes took in his thickly muscled shoulders and steely forearms, something seemed wrong, but he couldn't put his finger on it.

The man grinned suggestively. "She's quite a pretty package, isn't she? It came as quite a surprise to everyone that she could cause all this trouble." His eyes gleamed with a dangerous, lascivious light. "But I like a woman who puts up a fight. It adds spice to the encounter, wouldn't you agree?"

Dan felt a raw impulse to knock the sardonic expression off the bastard's face. As he shot an incautious fist toward the man's leering grin, the gun crashing down on the back of his skull brought stars. He swayed, grabbing onto the wall for support, refusing to let his body crumble to the Oriental rug underfoot.

"Don't be in such a hurry, my friend," Dan's intended victim advised, his voice menacing. "We want to leave him conscious enough to tell us where the film is."

As Dan watched, his smiling mouth twisted with a dangerous malice. "I'm growing bored with this conversation. If you don't tell us, I'll have to let Werner force the information from your girl friend."

He met Dan's blistering gaze with the unblinking eyes of a reptile. "Werner has one unpleasant little quirk—he enjoys inflicting pain on women . . . Need I say more?"

There was an implacable cruelty in the man's eyes that

Dan found as disturbing as Werner's alleged maniacal tendencies. He couldn't let either one of those men get to Jenny.

"The film isn't here."

"You're lying."

"Do you think she'd be stupid enough to hide it in her own house with you two goons after her?"

He felt Werner prepare to lower another crushing blow, but the man in charge held up a hand. "Be patient," he warned. "It won't serve our purpose if you kill him before we find out where she's hidden the film."

"I don't like being called a goon," Werner mumbled under his breath.

Cold eyes moved slowly over Dan's face as the man appeared to be making a decision. "Neither do I, my friend, but he'll pay for that little slur in due time."

"I told you, the film isn't here," Dan repeated with more insistence.

"Then tell us where it is."

"I'll take you there," Dan countered, deciding to get these two men as far away from Jenny as he could.

The man rubbed his jaw thoughtfully, his gray eyes flicking about the room, never really lighting on any one thing.

"Both of you have already led us on quite a wild goose chase. We expected her to have the film with her when she arrived in Sacramento. Imagine our surprise when a search of her briefcase and purse turned up nothing."

"Imagine," Dan murmured.

"Naturally, we assumed she'd hidden the film in her office."

"Naturally," Dan agreed, his mind going into overdrive as he tried to imagine what kind of film they were talking about.

"But our search turned up nothing."

"So you came here. Sorry, fellas, looks like strike two. One more and you're out."

Dan felt Werner tense behind him and knew he'd pushed too far. "Look," he offered in a burst of inspiration, "whatever you're being paid for the film, I'll double it."

Cold dark eyes flicked over Dan's gray suit. "You don't have that kind of money."

"I can get it."

There was a long pause as both men obviously considered the offer. Finally, Dan knew his time had run out when the serpent man shook his head. "I don't trust you; and I don't like you. I think it's time you and Werner became better acquainted."

Dan was suddenly spun around, his arms grabbed from behind by the muscle man, holding him face-to-face with the murderous Werner. Lance had been right, Dan realized, eyeing the man. It looked as though someone had stuffed a Neanderthal into that wrinkled suit. There wasn't going to be any easy way out of this.

"Any time you want Werner to stop," the second man advised, "simply tell us where you've got the woman hidden away and I'll call him off."

Dan bit his lower lip and stifled an instinctive moan as one huge fist buried itself into his midsection. "I thought you wanted the film," he managed in a weak gasp of air.

"That was before you made the mistake of not cooperting," the man replied. "Now you've forced us to deal directly with the woman. Something tells me we can convince her more easily."

The floor tilted as Werner's fists crashed down on his head. Dan tried to jerk away, but the other man's knee jabbed into his back, reminding him that he was outnumbered.

"Where is she?"

Dan shook his head, refusing to answer as the next blow brought a monstrous bolt of pain to his body.

"You can spare yourself all this," the dark voice crooned in his ear. "Just give her to us. She can't mean that much to you. No woman is worth dying for."

At one time Dan would have agreed. Even now he wasn't sure he was doing the right thing. Like Max Harte, he'd never been afraid of death, he just didn't want to be around when it happened, and he sure as hell didn't want to die right now. But he wasn't about to let them know where Jenny was, either.

He saw the flurry of fists coming, but was held helpless as Werner hammered at him with huge, malletlike fists.

"Damn it, man, just tell us where she is!" the voice yelled in his ear.

Dan only allowed a grunt to escape between his clenched teeth. He shook his head, experiencing a shaft of pain behind his eyes.

"You know we'll find her. And what Werner is doing to you will seem like a picnic then."

The idea of that gorilla touching Jenny caused Dan's mind to explode with fury. He jerked suddenly, freeing himself and throwing a punch at the man who had dared to threaten her. Caught in a cataclysm of hostility, Dan was beyond caring that his enraged counterattack could only prove futile.

Werner caught him by the back of the jacket, flinging him against the wall. Dan managed to roll away, but a well-placed kick crunched heavily into his rib cage and he lay on his back, his mouth open and his eyes shut, gasping for breath.

He felt the cold metal against his temple, just as he heard the click of the trigger. Dan realized with a detached sort of pragmatism that he was going to die and found it interesting that his last thoughts were going to be of Jenny Winslow. She was so lovely, so soft. In a form of mental escape he recalled the sweet scent of her hair, the lovely skin, the delicious taste of her lips, and the sensual way she'd trembled under his touch.

So lost was he in his erotic fantasy, Dan neglected to hear the screen door of Jenny's town house open.

"I saw you, young man! I saw you park your car in front of my house, thinking no one would notice you were sneaking over here. We've got a block watch program and don't allow thieves in this neighborhood!" The high-pitched, reedy voice infiltrated his consciousness, and as the two men cursed under their breath, Dan realized he'd just been granted a reprieve.

"We'd better get the hell out of here."

"What about him?" Werner sounded as if he hated leaving the job undone.

"We'll finish with him later. Right now we need to get out of here before the old broad calls the cops."

"But this guy can finger us."

They were already on their feet and Dan could hear them moving across the room, still arguing. "Hell, the chick may be crazy, but not crazy enough to let him go to the cops. Not after pulling that double-cross!"

Dan's headache was sharp, needling him with bursts of pain as he struggled to his feet. There was a dizzy, spinning nausea in his stomach and he reached out, grabbing hold of a chair to maintain his balance.

"Oh, dear me!" The elderly woman's mouth dropped open as she stared at him, her eyes huge.

"Please," he managed through clenched teeth. "Let me explain."

She was gone before he could make his case and, afraid

she'd gone to call the police, he knew he had to leave before they arrived.

His gut instinct had been right all along; Jenny had her own reasons for not bringing the police into it, but what double-cross were they talking about?

Dan moved slowly toward the doorway, fighting back a sour taste in his throat.

"Terrific," he congratulated himself. "Now, do you think you can make it to the car without embarrassing yourself by fainting or throwing up all over the sidewalk?"

Of course he could. It was simply a question of mind over matter, Dan assured himself as he staggered toward the red Corvette. A few pedestrians moved closer to the edge of the sidewalk, but seemed to take the sight of a battered, unsteady man in stride. Glancing down at his torn and bloodstained suit, Dan realized they simply took him for one of the derelicts who inhabited the downtown area.

He said a silent prayer that the car keys would not be buried in some hidden pocket of his suit and he was rewarded as he pulled them out on the first try. After unlocking the car, he settled his bruised body into the bucket seat with a deep moan. He tested his luck again and found it turned against him as he failed to locate his cigarettes. With a mighty effort, he leaned across the small interior of the sports car to open the glove compartment. It was as neat as he'd expect it to be, considering that Jenny had chosen a male alter ego for a partner. But at least the guy smoked, Dan noted gratefully, pulling out a fresh pack of cigarettes. They were menthol, but at this point, he wasn't in any position to be picky.

He lit the cigarette with shaky hands, started the engine, and managed to steer the car toward Nob Hill. He was reacting solely on instinct at the moment, headed toward Jenny with the tenacity of a homing pigeon.

"Oh, my God!" Jenny's hand flew to her mouth as she opened the door to Dan, supported on either side by red-jacketed bellmen.

"The manager offered to call the police, ma'am, but your husband insisted he'd be all right." The younger man's tone held doubt.

Jenny's appraising gaze swept over Dan. "Let me get him undressed and I'll decide what to do."

"It's a pretty bad mugging." The second bellman offered his opinion.

Dan stifled a moan as they helped him to the bed nearest the door. The first pulled down the spread while the second slowly lowered him to the sheets.

"Thank you," Jenny said. "I'm afraid I've misplaced my purse, but—"

"Don't worry about it," they both said in unison. "We're just sorry your honeymoon is going to be ruined."

"Honeymoon?"

Dan kept his eyes closed as he heard the surprise in Jenny's voice.

"Uh-oh," the first man said. "Now you've gone and done it."

"I thought it was just a secret to anyone trying to find them," the second man defended his words. "After all, Mrs. McGee knows it's her honeymoon."

"You're supposed to keep your big mouth shut, dummy."

They were still arguing as they left the room.

"When I checked in, I told the desk clerk we were hiding from friends who loved to play wedding night jokes," Dan explained.

"I don't care about that. What on earth happened to you?"

"If you think I look bad, you should see the other two guys." Dan managed a weak grin.

"Two? Were they the ones who've been chasing us?"

"No, these were the thugs Lance told us about."

"They were at my house?"

"Uh-huh. They tore the place apart, I'm afraid."

"That doesn't matter. I'm worried about you," she said reaching down to lift his shoulders from the bed so she could take off his jacket.

"I'm fine. Nothing's broken. Honest," he insisted at her skeptical expression.

"Well, I suppose one good thing has come out of all this."

"What's that?"

"This suit. It's finally beyond redemption."

Dan laughed, cringing as a hot pain seared through his ribs.

"Lie still," she directed, her fingers busy with the buttons of his shirt. He heard her sharp intake of breath as she observed his bare chest.

"That bad?"

"It's not good. I think we should call a doctor."

He caught her wrist as she went to leave the bed. "Wait a minute. Let me try to sit up."

"I don't think that's a very good idea."

"Trust me."

"I do," she whispered, and he knew it went far beyond the state of his health. "Oh, Dan, I'm so terribly sorry." Her fingers trembled as they traced the planes of his face with a touch as gentle as drifting snowflakes. "Your poor face."

He tried for levity, hoping to bring a smile to her tight, quivering lips. "That can only be an improvement."

"Don't joke about this," she replied firmly, eyeing him with a sober gaze. "I'm calling a doctor."

Dan shook his head, cringing as boulder-sized rocks tumbled across his brain. He couldn't forget the man's last words about Jenny's unwillingness to call the police.

Double-cross, he'd said. What the hell was she mixed up in?

"Don't do that. He'd probably have to file a police report and the last thing we need right now is to draw any attention to us. All I need is some aspirin and some sleep and I'll be as good as new."

"But—"

He pressed his fingers against her lips. "It's not the first time I've been beaten up while tracking down a hot story, honey. Believe me, the bruises fade, the aches and pains eventually go away, and before I know it, I've forgotten what it felt like to be used for a punching bag."

She left the room for a moment, returning with a glass of water and three white tablets which she gave to Dan. "This is all my fault. If I'd gone to the house instead of you, this never would have happened."

"Thank God you didn't," he remarked harshly, thinking about Werner. "Don't you understand, Jenny? If you'd gone there you'd be dead now."

"Oh, God, Dan, don't you see . . . you could be dead. I'm sorry I ever got you into this. I'm leaving right now, before you get hurt any worse."

Every nerve ending in his body screamed in protest as Dan jerked to a sitting position. Her face came in and out of focus, but he forced himself to hold her gaze.

"You try to leave this room and you're going to force me to stop you."

"Look at you, you can barely sit up," she pointed out. "How could you stop me from trying to save your life?"

"Anyway I have to," he shot back. "Because my life isn't worth a plug nickle without you, Jennifer Winslow."

He'd never used her full name and it had the desired effect as she stared down at him, her heart shining in her dark brown eyes.

"This is crazy," she argued in a barely audible voice.

"You're telling me," he agreed. "But life is full of crazy twists and turns, Jenny, and right now all I want to do is pass out for a little while without worrying that you'll be gone when I wake up."

She slowly lowered herself back down to the mattress, combing the blood-matted curls away from his wide forehead. "I'm not going anywhere," she promised. "Not without you."

"Promise?"

"Cross my heart." She made the gesture with trembling hands and Dan was grateful she didn't finish the childhood quotation.

"Jenny?" he whispered, lowering his head back to the down pillow.

"Yes, darling?"

"I think I'm going to pass out now."

The last thing he thought he heard was Jenny professing her love, but as he drifted off on waves of pain, Dan decided it must be wishful thinking. It was a nice thought, though.

His blinding headache had settled down to a steady dull throb when he awoke, his eyes opening to meet Jenny's fixed gaze.

"How are you feeling?"

He tried a grin that ended up a little lopsided. "Better. Have you noticed one of us is always waiting for the other to regain consciousness? There has to be an easier way to manage a romance."

"You're going to live," she diagnosed, managing a weak smile of her own.

"Of course. There was never any doubt," he lied. He moved to sit up, but Jenny was faster, her hands pressing him back against the bed.

"You're not getting out of that bed until I say so."

"Now that's the best invitation I've had in a long time. But I really need to get out of bed, honey."

"No way." She folded her arms over her chest. Dan noticed she'd changed into the long white gown and decided it must be night.

"Jenny," he coaxed, "be a nice lady and let me out of bed."

"You've been through a lot, McGee. Right now I'm calling the shots. And I say you stay put."

"Then we've a slight problem, darlin'."

"Oh?" She arched a disinterested brow.

His blue eyes moved toward the bathroom. "There are certain things even I can't control forever."

Her gaze followed his. "Oh. Well, all right. But then I want you right back in this bed."

He struggled to his feet, his smile wider this time. "You'll be getting no arguments from me on that score, Jenny, my love."

Dan forced himself to walk upright, not permitting the moans he felt rising in his throat to escape his lips. Jenny's beautiful dark eyes had revealed both concern and guilt and he wanted to spare her any further distress. He was relieved to find that the brutal punches had not damaged his kidneys, although a glance in the mirror told another story. His bottom lip was cracked, his skin was mottled with dark, ugly bruises, and there was a dark scrape along his cheekbone which he vaguely remembered being caused by Werner's signet ring.

While Dan had never thought of himself as handsome, at least until today he hadn't looked like Frankenstein's monster. Heaving a deep, somewhat painful sigh of resignation, he returned to the bed under Jenny's unwavering gaze.

"You undressed me while I slept, huh?"

An attractive color rose in her cheeks. "I was simply checking for broken bones."

"Makes sense," he agreed pleasantly. "You didn't by any chance take advantage of my unconscious state and ravish my body, did you?"

"Of course not!"

He sighed. "Oh well, a man can always hope. Although in a way I suppose I'm glad. When we do make love, Jenny, I want to be awake so I can remember every delightful detail."

Her eyes suddenly gleamed with a dangerous, lambent flame. "Exactly how sore are you?"

"That depends. What do you have in mind?"

"According to all laws of chivalry, when a knight defends a lady, he's entitled to a reward."

"I believe that's for slaying dragons."

"Only dragons?"

"If I remember correctly. Of course, I've been through quite a traumatic experience. It could be that I'm suffering from loss of memory."

"That must be it," she murmured, her lips brushing his with a light, delicate touch that stimulated without harming his split skin. "Because you've obviously forgotten that when a knight in shining armor saves his lady, he's stuck with her for life."

"You've already stripped off my armor," he pointed out, drawing in a sharp breath as her teeth nipped his earlobe. "Besides, I think that's a Chinese proverb."

"It doesn't matter," she declared loftily, "because we're stuck with each other, McGee, whether we like it or not."

He groaned as her lips played with the taut muscles of his neck.

"Oh dear, does that hurt? Should I stop?" Her breath was

like a gentle summer breeze against his skin and Dan felt himself warming with arousal.

"No—to both questions," he managed to say between clenched teeth as her thumbnail idly brushed against his chest, teasing his nipple.

The very idea that his body could respond this way only aroused him further. Dan had performed this identical act on countless women, receiving masculine satisfaction at their instinctively passionate response. But never had a woman taught him as much about his body as Jenny was doing now. He had never been this affected, never felt so involved, so committed.

"Does it hurt when I do this?" she inquired, her nail flicking with more determination, causing sparks to flare from deep inside his dark male bud.

"Jenny, I only have so much self-control," he warned as an answering passion surged through his loins.

"But Dan, I have to make sure nothing's broken . . . It's for your own good," she protested, throwing his own words back at him as her lips plucked at the other nipple. Dan pushed the soles of his feet against the sheet, lifting his body in mute need.

"Believe me, sweetheart, all the important parts are in working order."

Her dark eyes moved slowly down his body and a soft smile of feminine satisfaction curved her full lips. "So I see," she murmured, her fingers drifting through the ebony forest that covered his chest. "And such nice parts, too."

Dan thought he heard Jenny laugh, a throaty sound that was half honey, half smoke, but then she brought her mouth back to his, her tongue slipping deliciously between his lips to stroke the sensitive skin within, destroying coherent thought.

Chapter Nine

Dan had fantasized about making love to Jenny Winslow from the moment he had seen her, but never in his wildest dreams had he thought he could feel this vulnerable and defenseless. While she set about seducing him, his blood warmed wherever her hands fluttered over him and he heard his own deep moans as her lips followed the feathery path forged by her fingers.

She swept him into a realm of sensuality, where the only things that mattered were the tender touch of her hands, the sweet taste of her lips, the erotic scent of her own building desire.

She had the touch of an angel, expunging pain wherever her delicate fingers lingered, while her lips possessed the power to vanquish the soreness in his bones, replacing it with a pulsating, throbbing ache of need.

Dan's own hands were cruelly impeded by her nightgown and he breathed a sigh of relief when Jenny rose from the bed. Unselfconsciously lifting it over her head, she tossed it carelessly onto the floor without a backward glance.

She was so beautiful, tall and slender, her breasts rimmed with rosy aureolas tipped by taut, dark buds. Her hips flared outward from a slim waist and her tightly muscled thighs revealed a dedication to exercise. At the thought of those firm legs wrapped around his hips, Dan's blood thickened.

"You're beautiful." He breathed the compliment aloud, wishing that his writer's mind could come up with something less banal, something more suited to the vision standing before him. Jenny Winslow redefined the word "beauty," and for once in his life, Dan found himself at a total loss for words.

"You're prejudiced," she answered with a warm smile.

"No, I'm not. You're perfect."

"Not perfect." She slowly turned around, displaying her back. "See?" she asked, looking over her shoulder. "A distinct flaw."

Dan's gaze followed her finger to the small dark mole on the back of her thigh, right under the curve of her firm bottom. Forgetting that only a few minutes earlier he'd found any movement difficult, he reached out and pulled her to him, pressing his lips against the erotically situated beauty mark.

"Perfect," he argued, turning her in his arms. "I want you, Jenny . . . I've never wanted any woman more than I want you."

He cupped her buttocks in his large hands, bringing her nearer, his tongue tracing wide, wet circles on the satiny skin of her stomach.

"You're supposed to be resting." She murmured the slight protest a little sadly. "I wanted to make love to you." Her fingers ran trembling paths across the width of his shoulders.

"You will, Jenny, my love," Dan promised. "But you're the one who insisted on everything being fifty-fifty, remember?"

"I wasn't talking about everything," she argued, her fingers clutching him more firmly as his tongue cut a heated swathe through the curly blond hair at the juncture of her thighs.

"Oh, my God!" Her legs trembled as he retraced the sensual path with biting little kisses. Even as her head shook in mute denial, Jenny moved her hips into his touch.

Dan wanted to savor this moment; he wanted her to experience pleasure she'd known with no other man. He wanted his lovemaking to expunge any past lovers from her mind, leaving her with nothing but thoughts of him. Desire was flowing off her in warm waves, and he boldly thrust his exploring hand between her thighs.

He'd heard her utter an amazing series of lies. The notion that she had lied to him reminded him that Jenny Winslow was a tantalizing enigma wrapped in a devastatingly alluring puzzle. Yet there was no way she could be lying about this; her body gave her away as she pressed her feminine warmth against his touch.

"You were right about two very important things, sweetheart," he rasped against her flesh as his tongue searched out the tender flashpoint his fingers had thrilled. "I did save your life and now you're mine."

Her nails were biting into the flesh of his shoulders but Dan could not feel the pain as he drank in her honeyed taste, inhaled her rich scent, felt her flesh flowing like liquid fire beneath his touch.

He'd never felt the need to possess a woman before, yet suddenly he found himself wanting all of Jenny Winslow—not only her body, but her mind and soul as well. As his entire world narrowed to center on Jenny's soft sounds of pleasure, her warm and trembling body, it no longer mattered what she was mixed up in. Because Dan knew he was never going to let her go.

He looked up, his body threatening to explode as he watched her. Her eyes were closed, her lips moist and parted, her honey-blond hair streamed down like a silken waterfall as she arched her back to bring herself into his stinging caresses.

"Whatever happens, you belong to me," he grated thickly, pressing his palms firmly against her thighs. "You're mine, Jenny. My woman."

"Yes, Dan. Yes!"

Her body was seized with a violent tremor, her short gasps of pleasure mingled with cries of surprise as Dan brought her to fulfillment. Her moist, satiny flesh went pliant in his arms, and he pulled her onto the mattress.

"I can't believe what you do to me," she sighed with a strange mixture of happiness and regret. She reached out and pulled him close. "Can you feel that? Even now? I never knew this was possible."

Dan experienced a burst of male pride as he felt the pulsing contractions of her body, still responding to his lovemaking. He'd never met such a woman; they were like lightning striking dry kindling in the forest, igniting with all the violent powers of nature into a blazing inferno.

Her fingers were playing lazily in his dark chest hairs and Dan groaned as her palms moved tantalizingly downward over his stomach. Slipping out of his arms, she rose to her knees, her lips covering his as she took him tenderly, but without hesitation, in her hands.

"Jenny, my lovely, mysterious Jenny," he moaned as the swirling fog of desire returned to cloud his brain. With a low, muttered cry of desire, he pulled her into his arms and then she was under him, their bodies pressed together in mutual need. Her lashes fluttered closed as he tangled his fingers in her hair.

"Look at me, Jenny," he instructed huskily. "I want to see your eyes when I make love to you." She hesitated, as if her lids were held down by the dark fringe of lashes resting on her cheek. "Open your eyes, Jenny," he asked again.

She slowly obliged and a wave of passion flooded over him as he saw the answering need in her wide, dark eyes.

"I don't think I can wait any longer," he apologized in a ragged voice. He wanted to make love to her for hours, until they were both limp with satiated passion, but his traitorous body was screaming for relief.

Jenny reached down to guide him. "Please, Dan. Please love me now."

She lifted her hips and unable to resist any longer, Dan surged forward, with far more power than intended. At Jenny's gasp of surprise, he froze.

"Jenny? Sweetheart? Did I hurt you?"

"Never, darling," she breathed, beginning to move against him like a warm, sensuous cat.

As Dan luxuriated in the feel of her tight velvet folds rippling to adjust themselves to his strength, he forgot his humiliation and pain at the hands of those hired thugs. He put away his doubts about Jenny's honesty, and his concern over her safety. All his thoughts were on pleasing her, loving her.

"Oh, Dan . . ."

She wrapped her satiny legs about his waist and almost immediately her body tensed and she was crying out his name. As Dan felt Jenny's sudden inner convulsions, he experienced a savage pleasure that he could bring her to climax so fully once again. Then, even that primitive satisfaction was forgotten as his own release erupted with an explosive force, hurling him into a darkened well of temporary oblivion.

Dan woke with Jenny in his arms. She was still asleep, soft little breaths of air escaping her lips, and he felt free to examine her at his leisure. She was so slender, so delicate. From the beginning she'd seemed so fiercely independent, but holding her like this he was forced to wonder if Jenny would be strong enough to survive the dangers stalking her.

In the secret shadows of the night, she'd held nothing back, opening herself to him again and again, accepting his need as he answered with one just as desperate, just as intense. Her eyes were closed now, but their soft brown glow was burned into all his memory cells and he wondered how anyone with eyes so revealing, so filled with loving emotion, could be involved with men like Werner and his treacherous partner.

His Jenny belonged to a gentler place and time, where soft spring breezes ruffled meadow grasses and bright yellow daisies perfumed the air. A place of blue skies, puffy white clouds, and mellow sunshine. Try as he might, Dan could not picture her in a world where life and death had a price determined by the highest bidder.

He shook his head, turning his gaze to the ceiling, as if seeking answers in the white plaster. What was it about Jenny Winslow that made her so different from other attractive, intelligent women he knew? Was it the fact that she was, undeniably, a mystery lady who'd landed him smack in the middle of danger and intrigue? She reminded him of the beautiful blonde who always showed up in Max Harte's office, wearing her inscrutable secrets like a dark cloak. Oh, yes, this was definitely the stuff fantasies were made of and Dan had to admit he found the situation stimulating.

But if that was all there was to their relationship, why did he find himself feeling so protective toward her, so caring? Despite the stiffness in his joints and the dull ache radiating throughout his body this morning, despite the fact that he felt as if he'd been to hell and back, Dan would have willingly taken on a legion of hit men if it had meant shielding Jenny from a single moment's pain.

And the sex. God, the sex! She'd made him feel young again, and not just physically. The feelings he had while making love to Jenny took Dan back to those long ago days before he'd grown jaded, when he possessed certain ideals, certain illusions, about how things could be between a man and a woman.

Something in Dan's mind rebelled at the word "love"; logic told him love didn't come this fast, this hard. Love was an emotion that blossomed slowly, born of shared ideals, mutual trust and respect—areas where he and Jenny were decidedly deficient. He'd come to accept her amnesia as real, but Dan knew that she was deliberately hiding something from him. Something that had nearly gotten him killed yesterday.

Despite the knowledge that she was being less than truthful, everything about her filled his mind like a drug. It may not be love, but Dan knew he was hooked on Jenny Winslow.

Her sudden sneeze shattered his introspection. "The pillows," she explained, breaking into a series of violent sneezes. Dan reached out, grabbing a handful of tissues from the box on the bedside table.

"Thank you," she gasped, blowing her nose. "I'm allergic to down," she reminded him.

"That doesn't make any sense," he objected. "You slept in this bed with me all night and didn't sneeze once."

"Ah, but my body can only concentrate on one thing at a time. And you were marvelous at keeping it occupied with far more pleasurable matters."

Dan looked down into a face that could only belong to an angel and as he covered her soft lips with his, he turned his back on their dilemma, settling for whatever Jenny was willing to offer right now.

"Mmmm, you sure are one great kisser," she sighed happily as they came up for air. Her palms cupped his jawline and she pressed a stinging series of brief kisses against his darkly bristled skin.

"I should be jealous of all those women you've known. But if all that practice made your lovemaking so perfectly delicious, then I suppose I'm grateful."

"It's you," he admitted, wanting her as badly this morning as he had last night. As his palms traced her slender curves, Dan knew he'd never get enough of her. "You make me feel young again, Jenny."

Her silvery laugh was tinged with a slight note of inner regret. "Young? From the way you looked when you were dragged in here yesterday, McGee, hanging around me aged you in one short afternoon!"

"Would you do me a favor?"

"Anything," she answered promptly.

"Don't call me McGee when we're making love. Call me Dan, Daniel, sweetheart, or darling—anything but that."

Bert Brown, Dan's editor at *Newsview* always called him McGee, and the mental vision of that round, balding man with the scathing tongue, acid wit, and cheap cigars did nothing to instill desire.

Her eyes lit with a bright fire. "Is that what we're doing? Making love?"

Dan ran his fingers down her side, rewarded by her slight, involuntary tremor. "Got any other plans for this morning?"

She put her arms around his neck, drawing his head down toward hers. "None, Dan." Her lips plucked at his. "Daniel." She fit her body against his as she punctuated her words with short, hard little kisses. "Sweetheart . . . darling."

Dan's answering laugh was smothered by her lips as she led him to a brightly lit world of heightened emotions where reason and logic were swept away. His past became a vague, distant memory, nothing more, and the shadowy future held no meaning. There was only now—only this moment of shattering intimacy.

Much later, Dan forced himself to leave the bed, taking a solitary shower he longed to share with Jenny. But if he was going to take care of her, he was going to have to preserve his strength. And standing under the stream of warm water with Jenny was certainly no way to do that. He swore, twisting the knob to cold and scrubbing the bar of soap over his body with a force that was painful to his bruised flesh, but did nothing to lessen his desire.

Jenny smiled up at him as he exited the room. "We're going to be very rich," she announced.

He arched an inquiring eyebrow. "Rich? Is this where you tell me you've just remembered that you robbed Fort Knox last week?"

She had thrown the pillows onto the floor and was supporting her head with her arms. "Rich," she repeated, wrinkling her nose at his outrageous suggestion. "Since I never sneeze while you're making love to me, we've obviously discovered a cure for allergies. Now all we have to do is figure out how to bottle it and we'll make a bundle."

She smiled, a warm, satisfied expression, as her gaze swept over him. "Has anyone ever told you that you look very sexy without your clothes on?"

Damn her, anyway. Didn't she know what she was doing? He reached for his cigarettes but she was faster, holding the pack just out of reach while her eyes returned to their leisurely tour of his body. Dan stifled a groan.

"You smoke too much," she said.

Dan fought to keep his voice steady as he yanked on a pair of jeans. "You worry about your lungs, I'll worry about mine."

She sighed prettily, getting up on her knees to slip a cigarette between his firm, harsh lips. "Here. Far be it from me to deny the great Dan McGee anything he wants."

She was too damn close to him. He could feel the warmth of her body, feel her thighs pressing lightly against his as she flicked his lighter and brought it to the tip.

"You really have a magnificent build, Dan. Most men look better in suits; it gives them an air of authority. But your nude body takes a woman's breath away. You remind me of those marble statues of the ancient Greek athletes I've seen in museums. Until meeting you, I always thought those men were an idealized fantasy."

Dan didn't know which he wanted to do more—wring her lovely neck or return to bed and take her in a glazing whirlwind of passion before common sense could intervene. He bit right through the cigarette and Jenny appeared unperturbed as she picked the glowing end off the bed and stubbed it out into the ashtray.

"I love your body, Dan. And I love how it makes me feel."

The unpleasant thought that he'd simply served as an instrument of her sexual satisfaction burned its way to the front of his brain.

"I never thought of myself as a sex object." He shrugged in a poor charade of nonchalance. "But, whatever turns you on is fine with me."

Jenny put her arms about him, pressing her cheek against his chest. Her breath was warm against his bare skin and Dan felt his rebellious body stirring, coming alive with need. What the hell had happened to his self-control?

"Don't make it out to be less than it was," she requested softly. "It was infinitely more than sex, and you mean much more to me than you seem to think.

"You were right about my facade, Dan. I'm a maverick in a predominantly male field; I have to keep my emotions buried so I'm not accused of being an unstable female who can't make a rational decision one week out of every month."

He understood that. He'd seen cases where newsmen refused to go out on assignment in war zones with a female photographer for just that reason. He'd always thought it was silly, and had said so openly. But then, not every man had grown up with Lillian McGee for a role model.

Jenny's voice held a slight tremor. "I'll admit I'm afraid. I've been doing my best to be a good sport about all this, but I'm honestly scared to death. It's important for you to know that I didn't make love to you to forget anything that's happened. Anything that might happen.

"I fought hard for my independence, but meeting you has made me see that by insisting on total autonomy, I've denied myself the opportunity to love. To be loved."

Jenny's voice cracked a little, revealing that this was not an easy speech for her to make. Dan had never wanted to believe anything more than he wanted to believe this softly issued confession.

"Jenny, you don't have to tell me all this." He'd rather think of himself as a tool for Jenny's sexual pleasure than to be handed any false promises.

"I do," she insisted. "Because I've never felt so at one with a man before, Dan. It was as if I was lost, and in finding you, I've found myself . . . I wanted you, my love, for yourself—without excuses or regrets."

Her lips burned his skin as she pressed hot little kisses onto his chest, her hands moving like restless birds against the taut muscles of his back. Dan groaned as he combed his fingers through her tousled blond hair, knowing that in one minute her lovely lips would be creating both bliss and havoc with every nerve ending in his body.

"You'd better get dressed," he said on a harsh intake of breath. "It's not going to take those guys long to figure out that your partner's not driving his Corvette and start looking for us."

She sighed, running her palms regretfully down the back of his thighs. "I suppose you're right. It's probably difficult to make love encased in a body cast."

"Or worse," he reminded her grimly, images of Werner's sardonic smile as he'd repeatedly thrust his fist into Dan's body returning with an unnerving clarity.

"I'm taking you to my mother's," he announced the plan he'd come up with in the predawn hours.

"Your mother's? Dan, I didn't mean . . ." She looked decidedly embarrassed.

Dan felt a flash of irritation that, despite her charming little speech, Jenny was still unable to consider any sort of commitment.

"It's not what you're thinking," he replied brusquely. "She's got a cottage down the coast in Carmel. It'll be a safe place to wait out the return of your memory."

"Oh."

What the hell had he said now to upset her? "You'll be safe there, Jenny. Those goons obviously haven't figured out who I am; they won't make the connection."

"I hate all this," she muttered, leaving the bed. She frowned slightly as she pulled the pink dress from the closet. "You know, I truly love this dress, Dan, and I don't want to hurt your feelings, but I'm beginning to get a little tired of wearing it day after day."

He should have thought of that. Just because variety in a

wardrobe had never been important to him didn't mean
Jenny wouldn't want a change now and then.

"It's too risky to go back to your place," he apologized.
"But don't worry, I'll pick up something in the dress shop
downstairs while you take your shower."

"That place is bound to be expensive," she objected.

"You're worth it," he said simply.

She shook her head. "You're nuts, McGee." Then she
gave him a brilliant grin. "But you are kind of sexy, so I
guess I'll keep you around."

"Gee, thanks."

Dan suddenly remembered something he'd been meaning to ask her since he'd first gotten back from her town
house.

"Jenny?"

She turned in the doorway of the bathroom. "Yes?"

"May I ask a personal question?"

Her face shuttered momentarily, but the smile stayed on
her lips. "Sure."

"What are you doing with swords in your house?"

Relief flashed in her eyes, creating an icy knot around
Dan's heart. She had been expecting a different question
and he knew instinctively that she'd been prepared to lie.

"Errol Flynn forgot them after an afternoon of playing
pirate and kidnapped maiden," she quipped. "It's a fun
game, Dan. We ought to try it some time." Her gaze sparkled as it swept over his bruised body. "After you get back
into swashbuckling shape, of course."

"Jenny . . ." God, couldn't the woman ever give a
straight answer?

She laughed, dismissing his frown. "Didn't you ever
watch those old 'B' movies? Those aren't swords, McGee,
they're foils."

"Foils? As in fencing?"

She nodded. "My avocation. Actually, you could probably call it a secret passion; I work out at least an hour every day. Or I did before I started playing musical hotel rooms with you."

That explained her firm thighs, he decided, finding the idea that Jenny wielded swords—foils, he corrected—for fun far less surprising than he might have three days ago. He was quickly learning to expect the unexpected from this woman.

"You've got quite a few of those, don't you, sweetheart?"

"Foils? Only two."

"I was referring to secret passions. The longer we're together, the more I uncover."

Devilish lights danced in her eyes. "Complaining?"

"Not on your life."

He pulled a shirt out of the suitcase, shaking it to dislodge the network of deep wrinkles. When that didn't work, Dan put it on anyway.

"I'll be back in a few minutes," he promised. "Make sure you put the chain on this door."

"I will."

"And don't let anyone in."

"I won't."

Her dark eyes mirrored concern and he paused, his hand on the doorknob. "And don't worry about me."

"I will," she murmured, her eyes huge liquid pools as Dan managed to drag his gaze away and left the room before he gave in to temptation and spent the rest of his life making love to Jenny in a bed with down pillows that never made her sneeze.

Chapter Ten

"Tell me about your family," Jenny asked as they drove down the winding coast road. "After all, if we're dropping in on your mother without an invitation, I'd like to know what to expect."

"You'll like her."

Jenny smiled. "How could I not? Since I'm wild about her son."

That statement made him feel so good, Dan decided to believe it. "She's one of those people who always has a cause going. Saving baby harp seals, whales, that sort of thing."

"Maybe we should stop at a dress shop in Carmel."

Dan looked at her curiously. "What for? I've already told you Mom can lend you whatever you need for now." His eyes lit with a devilish gleam. "However, if I had my druthers, we'd forget the clothes entirely."

"Sex fiend." She grinned, but her dark eyes were soft with memories of their lovemaking. Then her expression turned a little serious. "Really, Dan, I want your mother to approve of me."

"She will," he responded instantly. "But what does that have to do with what you're wearing?"

His wide brow furrowed as the mismatched pieces suddenly fit into place. Lord, she was obviously picturing some silver-haired matron who spent her life planning fundraising balls. Dan laughed, a deep rich sound that reverberated in the small interior of the Corvette.

"Would you mind telling me what's so funny?"

"Honey, what's the first thing you noticed about me?"

"Your eyes," she replied. "They're the most gorgeous shade of Copenhagen blue. I thought they were an amazing contrast to your jet black hair. And your eyelashes." She sighed with exaggerated envy. "I know women who'd kill for those curly lashes, McGee."

Dan experienced a rush of adolescent pleasure at her words. "Are you blushing?" she asked, staring at him incredulously.

"Of course not!" It suddenly felt very warm, though. "It's just getting hot in here," he muttered, turning the air conditioner knob to a cooler temperature.

"You are too blushing, Dan McGee."

"What's the second thing you noticed?" He changed the subject back to its original track.

Again Jenny didn't hesitate. "Your smile. It's almost as gorgeous as your eyes."

Dan was honestly surprised. He hadn't thought she'd even noticed. Hot damn, he thought, inordinately pleased. He hadn't lost it after all.

"Want some more compliments?" she teased.

"Believe it or not, I was trying to make a point."

"If you want me to realize I'm in the company of an extremely sexy man, you've already proven that more than adequately."

"The suit. When did you decide my suit wasn't quite the height of fashion?"

"Oh." She thought back. "That came after the dirty book cover, but right before I spotted the gray in your hair."

"Gray?" Dan glanced quickly in the rearview mirror. "What gray? I don't have any gray hairs."

"Sure you do. Right here." She reached up, tugging at a jet black curl at his temple. "But that's okay; it gives you character."

"Those weren't there three days ago."

"Oh no?"

"Nope. I've obviously gotten them running around with you. So far in the past three days I've barely escaped being arrested, been chased twice by two mysterious guys in a black sedan, beat up by two other thugs who probably would have killed me if it hadn't been for your nosy neighbor . . . Hell, Jenny, by the time we solve this thing, I probably won't have a black hair left on my head!"

She ran her fingers through his dark curls. "That's okay. Then you'll be my silver fox instead of my sexy teddy bear."

Dan watched the warm, sensual memory coalesce in her eyes and wished they were nothing more than they appeared—two adults off on a romantic weekend at Carmel-by-the-Sea. But the magic elixir of Jenny's lovemaking had worn off and every aching bone in his body reminded him that nothing about their relationship was normal. It had as many unexpected twists and contradictions as the lady herself.

"We were talking about my mother," he remembered aloud. "Doesn't it stand to reason that any lady who'd raise a guy who dresses like me doesn't give a damn about superficial appearances?"

From her thoughtful expression, Dan knew Jenny was considering his argument. "You could always be rebelling against a childhood spent in Izod shirts," she reasoned.

"Nope. You're the rebellious one, remember? In fact, if you want to know the truth, Mom's been after me for living too carefully."

Jenny stared at him. "Are you kidding? I've read your stuff, Dan. There was that assassination attempt in El

Salvador, your expulsion from Moscow, and last year you tracked down a kidnapped diplomat in Paris, earning a death threat from the Red Brigade if you ever showed your face in the country again. You don't exactly lead a dull, country-club existence, darling."

"Spoken by the lady who designs buildings in Beirut," he murmured.

She shrugged offhandedly. "All right, so my work has taken me to some out-of-the-way places. At least no one was threatening to kill me."

"Oh no?" His dry tone was vaguely accusing.

"No," she stated firmly, her dark eyes turning a little hard as she pretended a sudden interest in the passing scenery.

Once again Dan experienced the discomforting impression that Jenny was holding back on him. He reviewed everything he knew about her, trying to find the key. As a young woman she'd needed more challenge and excitement than a southern Oregon cattle ranch offered. She'd ended up in San Francisco during the height of the flower generation era, ostensibly putting herself through college before immediately traveling to locations usually visited by only certain types of individuals: journalists, legislative members seeking headlines back home, mercenaries, and terrorists.

His unruly mind grabbed onto the last, making his heart sink. No, he argued with himself, he wouldn't believe that! But, try as he might to banish the disloyal thought, it continued to plague him. Finally, he pulled off the the road into the large parking lot of a cliff-side restaurant.

"I thought you might like lunch," he explained at her questioning glance.

Dan felt like a traitor as she gave him a lovely smile. "Thank you, I am a little hungry."

He mumbled an inarticulate response as he unfolded his large frame from the close confines of the sports car.

After they had ordered, Dan excused himself on the pretext of calling his office. Which was true enough, he simply neglected to add that he was calling for any additional information Marge may have been able to dig up.

"I'm glad you called," Marge said. "I've been worried to death about you."

"Worried?"

"Something really odd popped up."

"Odd?" Dan wasn't at all surprised.

"Well, we traced that license number you gave me. The car's licensed to the Sacramento FBI office. So, knowing you'd want more info, I plugged into the FBI data files and guess who showed up?"

"Jennifer Winslow."

"Those seem to be the secret passwords," she agreed. "Now the duck will come down and give you your hundred dollars."

"Could you just give me the information and quit playing around, Marge?"

There was a moment of stunned silence on the other end of the phone and Dan realized his gritty tone had not only surprised *Newsview's* chief librarian, but offended her as well. "I'm sorry," he mumbled. "I didn't mean to take all this out on you."

"All what?" Marge reminded him of a retriever who'd just spotted her quarry and was poised to flush it out.

"I don't know," he admitted. "But it's got me jumpy."

"Dan," there was no humor in Marge's voice now, "be careful. I don't like the looks of this woman's file."

"Why?" He pulled a cigarette from a crumpled pack. "What's in it?"

"That's just it—nothing. Except for that stuff I gave you the other day, the entire thing is classified."

Dan almost choked as he lit the cigarette. "Classified?"

"Yep. Not only that, but I called my friend in the bureau—you know, the one I use from time to time."

Dan didn't know the name of Marge's secret source, but he'd always privately referred to the guy as "the pipe." Whoever he was, the man had proven a reliable source of governmental leaks.

"What did he find out?"

"Nothing."

Dan felt himself sinking deeper into quicksand with each passing day. If he sank in over his head, would Jenny make a move to save him, he wondered.

"Nothing? Come on, Marge, the guy's got a finger in everything over there."

"She's got a special access code he can't break."

"Then tell him to find someone who can."

"It will be expensive," Marge warned.

Dan swore. "Look, I'm talking life or death here and you're worried about saving me a few bucks?"

Her tone was devoid of its usual teasing note. "I'm worried about you," she corrected. "Be careful, Dan. Whatever you've got going out there looks as if it could be big."

He muttered an agreement, gave her his mother's telephone number so she could reach him with any further information, and returned to their table.

Jenny smiled as he approached, making him wonder how anyone so lovely could be so treacherous. Dan didn't like to think that Jenny could be one of that near extinct group of urban terrorists who surfaced from time to time. Although most of the radical student movement of the sixties had turned in their placards and Maoist slogans for three-piece suits and keys to the executive washroom, there was still an

occasional bank robbery or bombing claimed by underground members of that radical fringe.

Not Jenny, he told himself firmly as he picked unchar-
acteristically at his meal. I won't believe it.

Still, his more rational self pointed out, what did he really
know about her after her arrival in San Francisco? She'd
attended college at Berkeley, certainly not a bastion of Middle America during that era. Then she suddenly began
popping up in Beirut, Iran, and South Korea. It just didn't
make any sense.

"Dan?"

He jerked his mind back to the restaurant as Jenny
reached across the table and covered his hand with hers.

"Are you feeling all right?"

"Of course."

"Are you sure?"

"I'm positive," he responded brusquely. "Ready to go?"

She looked at his plate. "You haven't eaten a thing."

"I forgot I'm allergic to shrimp," he lied quickly.

"That's crab," she pointed out in a tone that revealed she
knew he was disturbed and that she was the cause.

Dan heaved a deep sigh. "I'm sorry, babe. I'm just
worried."

"You can always leave, you know," she murmured, her
fingers trembling as they moved absently up and down the
stem of her wineglass.

"I told you," he stated with more force than necessary,
"I'm in this for the duration."

Her gentle brown eyes met his in a level gaze. "And
when will that be, Dan? Until your paychecks stop coming
from *Newsview*? Until you're finally beat up badly enough
to land in the hospital? Until one of us is dead?"

"Don't be stupid," he growled. The legs of his chair
scraped against the polished oak floor as he abruptly stood

up. "Nothing is going to happen to me. Or you. And in case you need clarification, Jenny Winslow, I'm with you until we get whoever is after you safely behind bars. I'm not leaving until I know you're safe."

Something unreadable flickered in the depths of her eyes for a moment, but it was gone before Dan could determine its meaning.

"Thank you, McGee. You're a good man." Her voice was barely above a whisper and she didn't look up at him.

There was so much more Dan wanted to say, so many questions he wanted to ask. Beginning with what she had been doing before they met that earned her a classified file at the FBI and ending with what she'd be doing the rest of her life.

"Ready to go?" he inquired instead.

Jenny managed a slim smile, but doubt still shadowed her eyes. "Ready," she agreed.

"Don't let my mother intimidate you," he instructed once they were on the road again.

"Oh, no. I think I'd rather take my chances with the thugs."

He chuckled. "It won't be that bad. Her usual method of intimidation is to test your shockability index."

"My what?"

"It's like her own personal Richter scale," he explained. "She always knows immediately how a person feels about her. If she senses disapproval, she drags out her worst behavior."

"Oh dear," Jenny murmured. "I'll try to radiate a positive reading."

"Don't worry, you'll pass with flying colors. I've got a gut feeling you two are soul mates."

Dan reminded himself that Lillian McGee could well be considered part of the radical fringe on environmental

issues. Some of her behavior was overtly illegal—witness
the little incident in Greenland when she'd thrown her
body over those damn harp seals. She continually espoused
activism and the need to stand up for one's beliefs, no matter what the cost. Was that so different from some of the
other movements, he wondered, searching for an excuse for
Jenny's possible misdeeds.

Yes, Dan admitted inwardly. His mother marched for
peace, embracing passive resistance. Lillian McGee fought
to ban the bomb; she could never make them in her base-
ment.

Could Jenny? he wondered, casting a surreptitious
glance her way. She was so wonderfully soft, so feminine.
But passionate, he reminded himself. Underneath that
cool, poised exterior, dwelt a woman of volcanic emotions.

She turned toward him suddenly, her smile wavering a
bit as she caught his intense study. "What about your
father? Does she intimidate him?"

"Dad's dead."

"Oh." There was a significant little pause. "I'm sorry."

"That's okay, you had no way of knowing. Besides, it happened a long time ago. And to answer your question, no one
intimidated my father."

"He sounds a bit like his son," she murmured thoughtfully. "Was he an activist like your mother?"

Dan nodded. "In a quieter, less flamboyant way. Dad
died in Mississippi during the freedom marches of 1962. He
was shot."

"By an allegedly unknown gunman," she finished, her
eyes coming alive with interest. "Dan, your father was John
McGee? The columnist for the *New York Times?*"

"You know the story?"

"*Everyone* knows that story. My God, he was a martyr to

the civil rights cause. I've read everything the man wrote during that time."

"You were too young," he argued.

"When it was all happening," she agreed. "But my best friend at Berkeley was a law professor who'd marched with him. She considered him a saint and had copies of every column he wrote for the *Times*. I think I must have memorized them all."

Her wide brown eyes sparked with a deep understanding. "No wonder you're such a white knight," she murmured. "How I envy you, having John McGee for a father . . . Tell me what it was like."

He shrugged. "I don't remember that much. Dad was gone most of those last years. But I used to watch on television and I can remember being afraid. Not just for him, but for everyone."

Dan's voice drifted off as he recalled, all too vividly, those years of turmoil. The scenes of the dogs, the fire hoses, those terrifying crosses blazing in the dark.

Jenny didn't say a word. She simply reached over and put her hand on his leg, stroking his thigh in a gesture that was meant to be comforting, rather than exciting.

"Whenever he'd come home, he'd scoop me up and hold me tight against his chest. He was so big and strong I let myself believe no one could ever hurt him. When he held me, I felt safe."

"I can understand that. Since it's the same way I feel when you hold me."

"Hey, watch out for my delicate male ego, sweetheart. I thought I'd inflamed your passions. At least a little."

The sensual smile she gave him took his breath away. "Oh, you do that, too, Dan. Magnificently."

"Daniel, how wonderful to see you!" The door to the

rustic little house was flung open and he was engulfed in folds of rainbow gauze. "But your face! What on earth have you gotten yourself mixed up in now?"

"It's good to see you too, Mom," he answered, ducking the question for the time being. "How were things in Greenland?"

"Let's just say that although the Greenland jails are nothing to write home about, I believe we made our point. And the world's a little safer for those precious baby harp seals. By the way, darling, everyone sends their thanks for the bail money."

"No problem," Dan murmured.

It crossed his mind that every member of the McGee family had been working to save the world in one way or another all their lives. He was growing weary of the burden. Let the world take care of itself for a while, he thought, all he wanted to do was to disappear to some tropical island with Jenny. That unruly thought led to an outrageous, but nevertheless attractive plan. If she was guilty of some international crime, couldn't he spirit her off to some remote locale that didn't practice extradition? Would she go? Dan shook his head, amazed that he'd even consider such a ridiculous scheme.

Lillian McGee's bright blue eyes looked past him to Jenny, who was standing silently in the background. "Well, are you going to introduce me to your friend or just leave her standing out there on the doorstep?"

As usual, Dan felt about twelve years old in his mother's presence. "Mom, this is Jenny Winslow. Jenny, my mother, Lillian."

Jenny extended her hand. "Hello, Mrs. McGee. I've heard a great deal about you."

"Call me Lillian. Mrs. McGee was John's mother. And a stiff-backed old harridan she was, let me tell you!"

"Mother!"

Lillian winked at Jenny. "Don't let him fool you with that high and mighty attitude," she advised. "Dan never liked his grandmother McGee, either. Especially after she boiled his pet sea turtle and served it up before the main course. Imagine!"

"Imagine," Jenny murmured.

Lillian linked her arms through both Dan's and Jenny's and led them into the house. "I'm so glad you've come to visit, darling. And how nice that you've brought your young lady."

"She's not my young lady," Dan protested automatically, not quite knowing how to explain Jenny's presence in his life. He regretted his words instantly when he saw a shadow move across her brown eyes.

Lillian watched the exchange, her eyes bright with interest. "I don't know what gets into my son at times, Jenny," she professed consolingly. "I certainly spent enough years teaching him manners."

He laughed at that. "In the first place, I doubt if you stayed home for six consecutive months during my first eighteen years, so any manners I may have picked up along the way were purely accidental." His eyes were smiling, assuring Lillian that he bore no grudges for her bohemian life-style.

"Are you two sleeping together?" she asked suddenly.

Jenny blushed a deep pink hue and Dan sighed, pulling out a cigarette. "Don't mind my mother," he advised dryly. "You've just got to get used to her and remember that no one ever takes her seriously."

"I beg your pardon," Lillian cut in testily, her irritation disintegrating as quickly as it flared. She dug through a pile of papers on her desk, smiling her satisfaction when she eventually located her own pack of long brown cigarettes.

"Where's it taken off to this time?" she muttered, riffling through the papers once again before disappearing from the room.

"I think I'm beginning to understand you, McGee," Jenny teased, her dark eyes bright with laughter.

Lillian returned before he could answer, the cigarette now stuck in a long jade holder which she shook at her son. "I'll have you know, Daniel Patrick McGee, that there are individuals—governments, in fact—who have learned to take me quite seriously. Even if you do insist on treating me as if I'm little more than an escapee from the road company cast of *Mame*."

"I just think that was a rather personal question, Mother, even for you," Dan pointed out.

Lillian shrugged. "Oh pooh, this is ridiculous. I was only asking because I only have two bedrooms in this cottage, and after those weeks spent on a filthy cot at the Arctic Circle, I'm not all that eager to give up my room, just for propriety's sake."

"One room will do," Dan stated.

As she clapped her hands, Dan noticed his mother was still biting her nails. "Oh, good. You've finally found a woman willing to put up with all your bad habits." She waved the cigarette once again in a warning gesture. "Just promise me you won't let the children call me granny. Or nana. God, that possibility freezes my blood!"

Jenny shook her head. "I think you've misunderstood the situation, Mrs.—uh, Lillian."

Blue eyes that were still as bright as sapphires observed the pair slowly, moving from Dan to Jenny, then back again. "No, my dear, I haven't," was her thoughtful answer. Then she grinned. "Dan, be a dear and bring in the luggage while Jenny and I get better acquainted."

"I've got my bag. Jenny's was stolen out of the car when

we stopped for lunch." Dan decided he was getting as proficient as Jenny at telling lies.

Lillian shook her head, clucking her tongue with regret. "Well, I'm sure it was some poor soul who needed the clothing more than us." She put her arm around the younger woman. "Don't worry, Jenny, you look about my size. We'll find something for you, although that dress is lovely. I was given a similar outfit by a gypsy I once traveled with. I was investigating human rights violations for Amnesty International and when my rented Mini broke down, the lovely woman offered me a lift in her motor home."

Lillian plucked at Jenny's full skirt. "Although my material was far coarser. This gauze is so summery, and the peasant neckline is perfect for your slender neck. You have excellent taste."

"Dan picked it out," Jenny offered, drawing a long, examining gaze from Lillian that made Dan instinctively want to shuffle his large feet.

"Well, Daniel, I'm impressed. Especially since you've always resembled a refugee from the Salvation Army yourself."

"You've never said one word against how I looked," he protested hotly.

"That's because I'm your mother, darling. I loved you before you had a stitch of clothing to your name. But if I'd been your lover, I'd have thrown away that horrid suit long ago. I suppose you still have it?"

"No. Jenny threw it away."

Lillian laughed, throwing her arms around Jenny. "I knew when Dan finally showed up with a woman, it would be someone I could love."

Jenny surprised Dan by returning Lillian's smile, but asking a pointed question of her own. "And if you didn't love her?"

Lillian lifted her rainbow clad shoulders in a graceful shrug. "I suppose it wouldn't really matter. Since I travel too much to visit my son very often, anyway." Her brow furrowed. "Speaking of that, you're not in the habit of dropping in on me, either, Daniel. What's up?"

"Can't a son visit his mother once in a while?" Dan hedged.

Lillian's expression revealed she wasn't buying his ploy for a moment. "You never could lie, Daniel. But I've never been one to poke into your personal affairs, so if you two will excuse me, I've got to get back to work."

"Saving the world for more seals?" Dan inquired dryly.

"You wouldn't think it so funny if you'd been born a baby harp seal," she retorted. "And no, for your information I'm in charge of our nuclear freeze rally."

Her eyes gleamed with a fervor Dan had witnessed countless times while growing up. "We're going to block the gates at Vandenberg Air Force Base with a continual chain of people, all holding candles. The light of reason," she elaborated, smiling at Jenny who smiled back.

"Damn it, that could end up getting you arrested again," Dan protested.

She nodded. "It probably will."

"Aren't you getting a little old for all this?"

Her blue eyes, mirror images of her son's, were solemn. "Daniel, as Edmund Burke said so eloquently, so many years ago, 'The only thing necessary for the triumph of evil is for good men to do nothing.'"

"I'm familiar with the quote, having grown up with it."

"Then you should know that I'm certainly not going to change at this late date." She pinned Jenny with a particularly sagacious eye. "Tell me, Jenny, where do you stand on this particular issue?"

Jenny spoke slowly, thoughtfully. "I believe we all have

to do whatever we feel necessary to make this a better world for everyone."

As Dan studied her somber expression he realized that she was not parroting words she knew Lillian McGee would appreciate. No, Jenny had spoken in earnest. Oh, Lord, he thought bleakly, what exactly did she consider necessary actions? He'd seen his mother pull some weird stunts, but to his knowledge, she'd never gotten in a mess as deep as the one Jenny was in right now.

Lillian, as expected, nodded her approval. "For once, Daniel," she said, exiting the room in a flurry of bright skirts, "you've shown some sense."

Jenny and Dan exchanged a smile. "You meant that," he murmured, hoping against hope Jenny would offer some simple explanation—like the fact that she bought savings bonds, or contributed to the Olympic committee.

"Of course," she said simply.

An expectant silence swirled between them. "How would you like to go for a walk along the beach?" Dan asked suddenly, wanting to put away the mantle of depression that was settling down around him.

"I'd like that."

"I'll be right back," he promised, heading off into another room and digging through Lillian's extensive cache of photographic equipment. After some searching, he located a thirty-five millimeter camera and a pair of binoculars that he hung around his neck.

"All ready," he announced, returning to her with a wide grin.

Dan and Jenny held hands, looking like nothing more than carefree lovers as they strolled along the rugged coastline. When they reached Point Lobos, Dan handed her the binoculars, pointing toward the offshore rock formations.

"Take a look," he invited.

Jenny lifted the binoculars to her eyes. following the direction of his arm. "Sea lions!"

"Or sea wolves, if you use the early Spanish explorers term," he agreed. "When I was a kid I used to sit on this beach and watch them for hours."

She smiled, her eyes warming with affection. "That must have been a lot more fun that watching some dumb old steers," she said with a certain envy.

"Wait until you see this."

He took her hand, directing her to the kelp beds floating offshore. Jenny laughed as the bewhiskered sea otters floated on their backs, using their stomachs for dining tables as they cracked shellfish open with flat rocks.

"I love them!"

"They were slaughtered almost to extinction during the 1800s for their fur. It was one terrific cause for rejoicing when a group returned to Carmel in 1938. I think that's when Mom made the decision to devote her life to helping others less able to take care of themselves."

He grinned as a butterfly flew past, its orange wings fluttering as it fought against the stiff sea breeze. "See that?"

She nodded. "It's a monarch, isn't it?"

"Yep. Anyone harming that bright little fellow is risking a jail term of six months or a five-hundred dollar fine."

"You're not serious?"

"It's true. Mother was part of the coalition who got that ordinance passed into law."

"Naturally," she murmured thoughtfully. Jenny looked up at him. "I honestly like your mother, Dan."

He put his arms about her waist. "You don't think she's a little strange?"

"Committed," Jenny corrected. "There's nothing wrong with being passionate toward something you believe in."

Dan lowered his head, his lips hungry for the taste of hers. "I'm a firm believer in passion," he whispered.

Jenny rose up on her toes, her hands going around his neck, her eyes bright with expectation as she prepared for his kiss. Suddenly, before either of them knew what was happening, Dan was thrown to the white sand and two dark-suited men were standing over him, their revolvers pointed at his chest.

"Don't move, McGee," the taller of the two men warned.

Chapter Eleven

"Are you all right, Ms. Winslow?" the man asked with a politeness one wouldn't expect from a hired killer.

"Who are you?" Jenny stared at the two men. "And why have you been chasing us?"

He reached into his breast pocket, extracting a slim identification case. The photo ID and the badge told them he was an FBI agent.

Dan's heart sank as he realized he was too late to save Jenny from these men who'd finally managed to track her down. He vowed that whatever she'd done, he'd hire the best lawyer he could find. And if that didn't work, then Lillian could damn well forget the seals and the rallys for a while and start a "Free Jenny Winslow" movement.

"Special agent Mike Flaherty, ma'am," the first man introduced himself. "And this is agent Brian Schneider."

The older man reached into his pocket and pulled out an identical folder that he opened in Jenny's direction. Neither his eyes, nor his gun wavered from Dan. "Pleased to meet you ma'am," he said. "Now don't you worry, we'll get this character into custody and then you can tell us your story."

"Custody?" Dan's roar resembled a wounded lion. "What the hell for?"

"Yes," Jenny inquired, her gaze moving from face to face

as she stared at the unlikely trio, "whatever would you want to arrest Dan for?"

"Kidnapping."

The terse answer hung in the air. Finally, Jenny probed a little deeper into this mystery. "Kidnapping?"

There was another long moment of silence. "Are you telling me that you went off with this man willingly?"

She blinked. "Of course."

"Just like that?" The second agent sounded even more irritated than the first.

"Not just like that," Jenny said, stiffening her spine. She suddenly reminded Dan of Lillian McGee and he realized he was not going to have anything resembling an easy or quiet life with this woman. "Only after he saved my life. On two separate occasions."

"You saved her life?"

The question was directed toward Dan, who'd been keeping quiet, trying to sort out this puzzling state of affairs. "Someone had to," he offered dryly, "since the FBI was out chasing phony kidnappers instead of following the real killers. What made you think I'd kidnapped her in the first place?"

Dan knew the men believed him when they put their guns back into their holsters. "Ms. Winslow never showed up for our meeting. The next thing we knew, we saw you driving out of the hotel parking lot with her in the car."

"That doesn't make me guilty of anything but taking a woman to a hotel room," he protested.

Flaherty shrugged. "You sure couldn't have proven that by the way you tried to ditch us."

"We thought you were the killers," Jenny explained, sinking down onto the sand. She looked up, an expectant expression on her face. "Well, at least now we're going to solve the puzzle. Why was I meeting you two gentlemen?"

They stared at her, then exchanged a glance. "You don't know? You're the one who contacted us."

"That's ridiculous. I don't know you."

"Rick Nichols contacted the agency and asked us to meet you at the White Horse Inn. He said he didn't know what it was all about, but you needed to talk to someone you could trust. He did say you told him you had evidence that could blow things sky high at several governmental levels." His gaze narrowed. "How come you don't remember?"

"Amnesia," she mumbled.

"But do you know who Rick Nichols is?" Schneider probed.

Dan watched Jenny's face turn a distinctly deep shade of crimson as she nervously sifted the sparkling sand through her fingers. "I know Rick," she admitted in a barely audible tone.

"Well I sure as hell don't," Dan felt obliged to point out. "And since I received what could very well have been a beating intended for the guy, do you think you could shed a little light on this problem, Jenny?"

She sighed, her eyes staring out at the sea gulls diving for fish in the ebbing tide.

"Jennifer? I'm waiting."

"He's my boss."

"Try again. You own your own firm. I've been to your office remember?"

Her dark eyes held contrition as she looked up at him. "I was really going to tell you, Dan. But, there never seemed a good time. And I really didn't think it had anything to do with Rick. I mean, I haven't done a job for him for more than nine months."

"What kind of job?"

She shrugged. "I'm kind of a free-lancer."

"A free-lance architect?"

Her hair fanned out from her shoulders as she shook her head. "Oh, Dan. This is so difficult. And it's not at all the way I wanted to tell you." Her gaze shifted to the two silent, observant men.

He squatted down beside her, taking her hands in his. "Look, honey, whatever you're going to tell me can't be any worse than some of the wild ideas I've come up with on my own. And I loved you in spite of them. I even loved you when I thought you were a terrorist."

"You love me?"

"Of course," he answered simply.

Jenny's eyes widened as she realized the rest of what Dan had said. A silvery little laugh bubbled up as she traced his jawline with her fingertips. "Oh, Dan. Did you really think I was a terrorist?"

"Well hell, Jenny, what kind of woman runs around Beirut these days? Or South Korea? Not to mention Iran. And your FBI file is classified, with the code damn near inaccessible!"

Her gaze was filled with admiration. "My, my, you have been busy. Another twenty-four hours and you probably would have uncovered my agency ties."

"Agency?" He arched a puzzled brow. Then slowly, comprehension dawned. "Oh damn. We're not talking FBI here, are we?"

"No," she admitted softly, "we're not. I'm afraid that what got these gentleman so upset is their belief you kidnapped a CIA courier."

"I think we'd better have a long talk," Dan said after a pause.

At the moment, he didn't know whether to laugh or cry. At least it was beginning to make some sense. He still didn't like it, but he decided it was probably better to love a lady spy than a lady terrorist.

She nodded.

He rose from the sand, jamming his hands into the back pockets of his jeans as he stared out at the Pacific, trying to choose his words carefully. He failed. Miserably.

"What the hell kind of woman works for the CIA?"

Jenny's back stiffened a bit at the uncensored accusation in his tone. "That's a loaded question."

His blue eyes were hard. "Maybe you're just afraid to answer it. I knew you were stronger than you looked, but my God, Jenny, a spy?"

She folded her arms across her chest. "You're letting that wild writer's imagination run away with you again, McGee. I don't run around the world bringing down governments or assassinating despots, for heaven's sake."

"That's a relief," he responded dryly. "So, what do you do?"

Dan returned his gaze out to sea, and heard Jenny's barely stifled sigh. Okay, so he wasn't being that easy on her, but damn it, how could she have kept a secret like this from him after all they'd been through together? Especially after last night.

"I merely serve as a pipeline for the flow of important information."

Still focusing on their lovemaking, an unruly little thought flashed through his mind. Dan discarded it immediately, but he was hurt enough to say the words.

"How, exactly, do you get this information? In the typical Mata Hari fashion—in bed?" He tacked on cruelly, just in case she'd missed the innuendo in his voice.

Jenny gasped and Dan instantly damned his unruly tongue for hurting her. He wanted to apologize, but pride kept him silent.

"That's a low blow, and I resent it. Not just for me, but for all the women I know who work at the agency."

God, she made it sound like something from a bad spy novel. Agency, with a capital A. Dan couldn't believe they were standing here, in one of the most romantic spots on earth, having an argument because he'd just found out the woman he loved was a spy. As furious as he was, Dan knew he was being too harsh with her. After all, he'd loved her as a terrorist, why couldn't he accept this latest development?

"I suppose my mother's to blame for this," he muttered, wondering what Lillian would say if she knew her future daughter-in-law worked for the CIA. Needless to say, Jenny's agency was not one of his mother's favorite charities.

"Lillian? How?"

"Her damn work with the woman's movement probably opened the door for you in the first place." He scowled. "That's a lousy job for a woman, Jenny."

"Of course it's a dirty job, McGee," she teased softly, putting her hand on his arm, "but someone has to do it."

Dan wasn't laughing. "Not you, damn it!"

Jenny tried again. "Dan, I have a friend who used to work for the agency. She's established an executive protection firm in San Francisco and her husband doesn't have any problem with what she did." Her tone grew softly coaxing. "Let me introduce you to them, and you can see that it doesn't have to have anything to do with us."

"Does she still work for the *agency*?" He imbued an extra heaping of scorn on the term.

"No," Jenny admitted softly.

"Will you quit?" Even as he asked the question, Dan knew he had no right. But he had to know.

"Humph." Mike Flaherty cleared his throat. "Look, could you two settle your little domestic differences some other time? We'd like to try to get this thing straightened out."

Jenny looked distinctly relieved by the change in subject.

"Of course," she answered instantly. "But I don't know how much help I'm going to be."

Flaherty's gaze turned to Dan. "You said you'd been beaten up?"

"No, I always look like this," Dan retorted, getting sick and tired of this entire farce. "It's not too bad; I pick up a few bucks from time to time whenever Hollywood needs an extra for their latest horror film."

"Film!" Jenny spoke out loud and all three heads turned toward her simultaneously. "I remember now. I was going to take the film to Sacramento, but at the last minute, I was afraid I was being followed. I hid it."

Her dark eyes brightened with sudden insight. "Rick arranged for me to meet with you. I was afraid to call the local FBI office, because I didn't know who I could trust. Rick assured me you were both honest and discreet."

"What was on the film?" Schneider asked.

Waves of distress washed across her face. Jenny's brow wrinkled into deep furrows as she closed her eyes, concentrating hard. "I can't remember that part."

"No problem," he assured her quickly. "Just tell us where you've hidden it, and we'll have the answer in no time."

The expression on Jenny's face told the entire story. "I'm sorry," she murmured sadly.

Dan's previous irritation melted like sugar crystals in hot tea. He put his arm around her shoulders, giving her a reassuring squeeze. "Hey, we're coming closer, honey. I'm sure it's only a matter of time."

"The problem is, we may be running out of that particular commodity," Flaherty pointed out. "If you could give us a description of the men who assaulted you, Mr. McGee, at least we'd have a starting point."

Dan nodded, debating whether or not to return to the

cottage. No, he decided, this would be far better kept from Lillian. "Do you mind if we talk here?" he asked. "It's more private than the house."

They agreed, pulling notebooks from their pockets on the first try. Dan secretly admired that ability and decided he'd never qualify for the job if that were one of the criteria. He described the two men as best he could, including the oddly British accent of the man who'd done most of the talking.

"Wales," he said suddenly.

"Whales?" Jenny looked out toward the water, and the two men's gazes followed hers.

"No. Wales. The country. The guy's from Wales."

Schneider nodded, appearing pleased as he scribbled the notation. "That should help," he commented. "Unless he's an illegal, he'll be in Immigration's files. Anything else?"

Dan thought back, remembering something had bothered him about the guy in the first place. "He's a professional body builder."

"How in the world do you know that?" Jenny looked at him with open admiration.

"The guy didn't have any hair on his arms. And he looked like a weight lifter."

"Piece of cake," Mike Flaherty grinned, sticking the notebook back in his pocket. "Even in San Francisco, there can't be that many professional Welsh body builders."

"I still don't understand," Jenny objected.

"A lot of body builders shave their body hair," Dan explained. "It looks better for competition when they get oiled up."

Brian Schneider pulled out a business card, handing it to Jenny. "Here's the office number, as well as my home. If you remember anything else, call us right away."

"I will."

"And you'll be staying with Mrs. McGee?"

Dan nodded. "I'm impressed with the way you discovered us so quickly."

"It wasn't that difficult," the agent shrugged. "But you did throw us for a while, dumping the rental car and picking up the Corvette."

"Lance is going to kill us," Jenny groaned.

Dan laughed. "We'll invite him to the wedding. That'll make up for it."

She shook her head. "Crazy, McGee. You are definitely off your rocker."

"I'm crazy about you," he agreed. "Ready to go back and face my mother?"

"I'm ready for anything," she promised.

"Daniel, wait until you see what I found!" Lillian was standing in the doorway, waving a large box as they approached. "The slides from the whale rescue."

"Whale rescue," Jenny murmured under her breath.

"Of course," Dan agreed. "And I think we're in for an evening of play-by-play."

Jenny sighed. "Oh well, I could never make love in the same house with your mother, anyway."

Dan bent down and kissed the nape of her neck. "Don't bet on it," he whispered.

They sat in the darkened room, holding hands and watching as Lillian flashed scene after scene of the Greenpeace mission onto the screen. As the Soviet trawlers neared the group's small boats, Dan admired his mother's courage and told her so.

"To tell you the truth," she admitted, "I think we were all too exhilarated to be frightened for our lives. I will admit to being afraid all these rolls of film would end up in the bottom of the sea if those horrid men swamped our boats."

She smiled with obvious pride. "But I got around that. I

put the film into Ziploc plastic bags, then hid them in a secret pocket on the inside of my life preserver."

Dan cringed as Jenny's fingers suddenly squeezed his with an unholy strength. "Jenny?" he asked under his breath as Lillian chattered on. "What's the matter?"

"It was right there for a minute," she whispered. "I almost remembered everything. But it was just like that first time in the hotel, I couldn't quite reach it."

"Don't worry. This will all be over before you know it and we can get on with our lives."

Her eyes gleamed suspiciously moist in the dark room as she looked up at him. "I'll give it up, Dan. I don't work that often, anyway."

"We'll talk about it later," he insisted.

She nodded and they returned their attention to Lillian's slides.

"God, I thought this moment would never come!" Dan muttered harshly, pulling Jenny into his arms.

They had dutifully watched all two hundred and forty seven slides, listened to anecdotes about every member of the Greenpeace team, and patiently sat through a lecture on the relative intelligence of whales compared to man. Now at last they were together in the privacy of Lillian's guest room, lying in the comfortable double bed, their arms and legs entwined in a loving embrace.

"Mmm," she murmured blissfully as his lips covered hers. "Your mother is a nice person, but after the hundredth slide all those whales started to look the same to me. I can't believe they named them all, and then were actually able to keep track which was which."

"My mother is a very unique individual," he agreed, his teeth nibbling at her lower lip, "just like the other lady in my life."

"Dan—" Jenny caught his hand as it moved up her thigh.

"Shhh." He tugged at the white nightgown. "Why did you bother to wear this thing, anyway?"

"Protection. I can't make love to you knowing your mother's in the next room."

He chuckled as he untied the blue ribbon, his hand slipping inside the neckline to cup her breast. "Darling, this little bit of cotton is not going to keep me from touching you." He bent his head, his warm tongue flicking at the hard pink bud. "Or tasting you."

"Dan, we can't," she whispered in a muffled moan as he pulled her onto his chest. The nightgown bunched up around her waist as he stroked her thighs. "Daniel, your mother is on the other side of this wall!" Jenny hissed.

"It just takes a little more ingenuity," he insisted. "I promise, we'll be very quiet."

Before she could object, he pulled the nightgown off, flinging it across the room. Her nude body gleamed in the moonlight drifting in through the curtain. As Dan's eyes drank in her beauty he knew he'd never tire of seeing Jenny this way, magnificently wanton, aroused with passion, her dark eyes gleaming with love.

"Ah, isn't this nicer?" His mouth captured her breast and as he suckled greedily, Jenny arched her back, unable to stifle a slight moan.

His lips covered hers, the kiss at first gentle, then increasingly passionate as their roving hands brought each other pleasure. With every movement of her mouth on him, Dan trembled, his desire for her more overwhelming than it had ever been.

Jenny whispered words of love, words of pleasure into his ear, and as he stroked and fondled her, Dan planted kisses, passionate kisses, all over her fluid body. He delighted in the way her skin bloomed under his lips, the way she shivered under his touch and the way she welcomed everything he did to her.

"Now," she whispered against his lips, rolling onto her side to face him and slipping one leg underneath him, the other over his hip. Dan plunged into her with a deep, rhythmic stroke, his mouth swallowing her soft cries that excited him to new heights of passion. Their lovemaking echoed the age-old force of the surf pounding against the rocks outside the open window as they rode the cresting waves of passion, giving completely to each other, holding nothing back.

Suddenly they were engulfed by a cresting, pounding wall of water that swept them into churning white waters. Dan clung to Jenny, his mind filled with the roar of the surf as they were flung into the creamy white froth, riding the tidal wave until they emerged onto sparkling, glasslike waters. Both blissfully content, they floated on the warm buoyancy, their lovemaking having been heightened by their recent commitment to one another.

Dan was lying on his side, leaning up on his elbow, gazing down into Jenny's flushed face. It amazed him how much he loved her, but what was even more amazing was that she loved him in return. Dan McGee was thirty-eight years old, but tonight he felt as if he'd been reborn, as if his life had just begun.

He was just about to tell Jenny all this when she suddenly sat up, her eyes brightening to gleaming jet in the moonlight.

"That's it!"

He pushed the soft hair away from her face with fingers that trembled slightly with leftover passion. "What's it?"

"Your mother's life preserver. That's the key!"

"Are you telling me that you were thinking about my mother while I was making love to you?"

She framed his frowning face in her hands, pressing a deep, reassuring kiss against his lips. "Of course not. But you know how afterwards, your mind just seems to float along, thinking of nothing in particular? Well, that's when it came to me. I know where the film is!" she exclaimed triumphantly. "Not only that, I remember everything!"

He gave her a hard, congratulatory kiss. "What did mom's life jacket have to do with your memory returning?"

"At the last minute I was afraid to take the film with me, but I've already told you that."

He nodded.

"So I tried to think of the one place no one would ever think to look."

"Jenny," he complained, "do you have to drag this story out so damn slowly? Where is the film?"

She grinned. "In my fencing vest. I cut open a seam and stuck the roll into the padding."

"Just like Mom did," he thought aloud. "God, I knew you two thought alike, but this is downright frightening."

"Come on," she said, ignoring his statement. "We've got to get back to San Francisco."

"Why don't we just call those FBI guys and let them handle it? What's on that film anyway?"

"I'll tell you on the way," she said, throwing the ivory gauze peasant blouse over her head.

"I still think we ought to let the professionals handle this."

"I *am* a professional," she replied levelly.

"Don't remind me," Dan groaned, raking his fingers through his hair as he got out of bed. "I keep trying to forget that little fact."

Chapter Twelve

In the end they compromised, calling the FBI agents before leaving. Unable to reach them at either the office or the house, they were forced to leave a message. Then, leaving a hastily written note for Lillian, they headed back to the city. As Dan drove up the coast, Jenny explained about the film.

"I was really excited when I got the job for Kennington Construction. I mean, those guys are worldwide. It was a terrific opportunity."

Despite his dark sense of foreboding upon hearing the name of the company involved in all this, Dan was impressed with Jenny's obvious skills and told her so.

"Thank you, McGee, that's very nice of you. Anyway, I was so thrilled about the high-rise I went by and took pictures at every stage of construction."

"Don't you usually?"

She shook her head. "Not always. As long as the buildings pass inspection and nothing goes wrong, I can't take the time to check each site every few days."

That made sense. "But you did with this one?"

"I went out after the steel went up. It had already passed code, but I wanted to see the building before the floors were poured."

"And?"

Her expression was solemn in the moonlit interior of the car. "And not only was a lot of the steel not up to spec, but on some of the floors there were bracing beams missing all together."

He shot her a quick glance. "Are you telling me that those floors could collapse?"

"It's possible under the best of conditions, but when we design buildings for this part of the country, we have to allow for tremors, too."

"And if there's an earthquake?"

"I don't have a crystal ball," she admitted. "But I'd bet that place will go down like a pile of building blocks."

He frowned. "But it passed inspection?"

She nodded. "The concrete was scheduled, so I immediately called up Kennington's office in San Francisco and talked to the superintendent, who brushed me off. Then I went down there and kept trying to convince the men in charge that they were going to have a real problem."

"And?"

"First they reminded me that they had a green tag on the steel."

"A paid off inspector," Dan guessed.

"And kickbacks on the steel, not to mention a very strange zoning change to allow the building in the first place. So, I went back to Kennington, telling them what I'd found."

"They weren't surprised." Neither was Dan.

She looked at him curiously. "No. Not only that, they offered me money to forget I'd ever seen the inferior steel."

"Which you refused." She was suspiciously silent. "Jenny, you did turn the money down, didn't you?"

"Not exactly."

"Not exactly? What the hell kind of answer is that?"

Her fingers plucked nervously at the material of her skirt.

"I was afraid no one would believe me. I mean, it was my word against the word of some very important people." She took a deep breath. "So, I hid one of those little tape recorders under my clothes and recorded the payoff."

"You tried your own sting? All by yourself? Damn it, Jenny, that fool stunt almost got you killed!"

"I think it was when I took the pictures that I got in trouble," she admitted. "I went out there on a Sunday, but a security guard saw me. He must have been on their payroll."

Dan realized this was the double-cross that had endangered her life and muttered a low, harsh curse. "You need a keeper."

She leaned over, kissing him swiftly. "I'm sorry. I realize now it wasn't the most prudent thing to do. But I needed proof to take to the authorities."

He combed his fingers through his hair, knowing he'd probably just acquired several more gray ones.

"There's more," she offered. "The brother-in-law of the zoning commissioner just happens to be State Senator William Thompson."

"The same William Thompson who was campaign manager for U.S. Representative Malcom Griggs, chairman of the House nuclear regulatory committee."

"How on earth did you know that?"

"It's the story I dropped when I met you. I was tracing it backward from some rumors that several of Kennington's nuclear power plants were being built with inferior materials. I was tracking a nationwide chain of kickbacks and payoffs by top Kennington officials." He shook his head. "Ironic, isn't it? We were both working on the same thing."

"Amazing," she murmured.

"The film, I take it, shows the steel before the floors were poured."

"Uh-huh."

An unpleasant thought suddenly occurred to him. "How the hell did you get the shots of the higher floors?"

Jenny looked at him with some measure of surprise. "How do you think? I went up there."

"You were climbing around on some oversized erector set? Hundreds of feet above the street?"

"That's my job," she remarked calmly.

"I think I hate that idea worse than the spying," he muttered.

She put her hand on his arm. "I want to explain about that, Dan. My last year of school I was serving an apprenticeship with an architect who was building a housing development in Egypt. He introduced me to a friend of his at a party."

"Who just happened to be over there carrying out covert activities. Illegal covert activities," he pointed out.

"Now you sound like your mother," she accused. "Look, all I ever agreed to do was to take messages out of certain hot spots to people who needed that information to protect our citizens overseas. If the administration had listened to us, there never would have been that mess in Tehran."

Her tone softened, becoming more conciliatory. "I wasn't lying when I told your mother we all have to do what we believe in. I know the agency's reputation gets a little sullied from time to time; I'll also admit they get carried away with some of their ideas. But I never did anything I'm ashamed of, anything I wouldn't feel free to tell you or your mother."

Dan knew she was telling the truth. He reached over to take her hand and bring it to his lips. "I believe you, sweetheart. But it might be better if we didn't tell Mom. She's guilty of tunnel vision where your precious agency is concerned."

Jenny nodded her agreement and they both grew silent as the car filled with a nervous expectation.

"Oh, my God!" Jenny stared at the shambles of her home. "Dan, look what they've done!"

Her bleak eyes took in the pictures ripped from the wall, their frames broken by the intruders who had searched behind the paper backing. The silk upholstery on her sofa had been slashed and the foam material of the cushions was strewn over the Oriental carpet like unmelted snow. All the books had been torn apart and pages were littered about everywhere.

As she slowly made her way to the bedroom, Jenny couldn't stifle a cry as she saw how her clothing had been flung about, and Dan was furious when he realized some of the silky underthings had been torn for no other reason than to give the vandal some sick pleasure. Werner, he knew instantly, gall rising in his throat. If he ever ran into that guy again, he was going to kill him.

"Sweetheart, let's just get the film and get out of here," he suggested gently. "We'll have someone come in and clean this mess up."

She was staring at a lacy, ecru slip, her fingers tracing the long rents caused by an unseen knife. "Why?" she whispered.

"Don't think about it," he insisted, taking the slip from her fingers. Her knuckles were white as she clutched the material. "The film, Jenny," he reminded her.

She shook her head, as if to clear away the distressing thoughts and returned to the small parlor, picking up the padded white fencing vest. "It's still here," she said, pulling out an undeveloped roll of film and a small tape cassette. "They didn't find it."

"You may be crazier than a bedbug, Jenny Winslow, but

you're also one clever lady," he complimented her, giving her a quick, hard kiss against her trembling lips. "Now, let's get the hell out of here before we get some company."

As she nodded, they both heard the squeak as her screen door was opened. Her eyes widened, meeting his with the obvious question. Dan knew Jenny was wondering the same thing. Who had just entered the narrow foyer? There were two obvious choices, and suddenly he felt like the man who was about to face either the lady or the tiger.

He pressed his finger to her lips in a silent warning, taking her hand and leading her to the wall next to the doorway. There was no time to escape out the back; they'd have to take their chances.

As the first man entered the room, Dan brought his fists down with all his strength. Whether it was instinct, or whether Werner had actually felt the air displaced by the movement, he ducked, and Dan cursed as his blow landed on the man's thick shoulder. The force dislodged the gun, and as it fell to the floor, Dan debated reaching for it. Knowing Werner would have the same chance, he instead kicked it down the hallway while at the same time driving his fist into the larger man's stomach.

"Ooof." Werner expelled a harsh breath, swinging around to push Dan against the wall. Lowering his head, he used it as a battering ram, pounding into Dan with a force that sent him reeling. He grasped hold of his assailant, pulling him to the floor where they rolled over the piles of Jenny's scattered possessions.

"Jenny," he managed to shout, as he emerged on top of the flailing man, "get the hell out of here! *Now!*"

But Jenny had made her decision even before she saw the second assailant materialize and reach for his own gun. Grabbing the foil lying on the cushionless sofa, she lunged, drawing blood from the Welshman's wrist. He cursed viciously as he bent to retrieve the gun he had dropped, but all Jenny's training served a purpose.

"Don't try it," she warned, advancing toward him.

His black eyes glittered dangerously as they shifted from the gleaming metallic foil in Jenny's hand and back to the gun. As Dan ducked, avoiding the uppercut thrown by the man beneath him, he saw the body builder make his decision.

"Goddamn it Jenny, run!"

With Dan's attention momentarily diverted, Werner regained the advantage and reversed their position. As he threw his hands up to protect his face, Dan prayed Jenny wouldn't attempt any heroics.

With flashing speed, Jenny plunged her foil tip into the back of the man's hand as he grabbed once more for his weapon. The unexpected pain drew a roar of anger.

"Do that one more time and I'll aim someplace more lethal," she advised him coldly.

"You couldn't kill a man." Knowing that these were the men who'd so brutally beaten Dan, she was forced to seriously consider the matter. "I wouldn't want to," she admitted. "But if you make one move toward that gun, I'll do anything I have to do to stop you."

His blazing gaze shifted to the two men engaged in a savage battle. "When Werner finishes with your boyfriend, I'm going to let him take his time with you. He's been wanting a chance alone with the owner of all those lacy underthings."

The man's venomous threat gave Dan a surge of adrenaline that let him alter the course of the battle once again. He jerked his knee up, feeling a satisfying crunch as he drove it into Werner's groin. The larger man rolled onto his back with a scream, clutching himself in agony. Blind with rage, Dan leaped on him, driving his fists over and over again into the man's already bloodied face.

"Dan! Dan, stop! Oh, my God, please stop. He's not moving!"

Through the roaring in his ears, Dan vaguely heard Jenny shouting and he shook his head, focusing on the limp body beneath him. His blazing gaze moved to the man whose back was pressed against the wall, his beady black eyes shifting from Dan and Werner to the foil Jenny was pressing against his throat.

"You want to be next?" Dan asked.

The man shook his head, sweat streaming down his face.

Dan reached out, having to uncurl Jenny's rigid fingers from the handle of the foil. "I'll take over now," he suggested softly, disturbed by the icy feel of her skin. "Do you have any rope?"

"Rope?"

"I think it might be advisable to tie these goons up, don't you?"

"I have some clothesline in the kitchen."

"Perfect."

She backed out of the room, her wide brown eyes locked onto Dan, as if unable to believe he was safe.

"I could kill you while she's out of the room," Dan suggested offhandedly.

"You'd go to prison."

"I'd just say it was self-defense. Let's face it, you two don't have such sterling reputations. Any jury in the world would take my word over yours."

"You're both crazy."

Dan nodded, smiling at that. "I've come to the same conclusion," he agreed pleasantly.

"And dangerous."

"Keep that thought." He pressed the tip a little more firmly into the man's skin. "Because if you, or any of your friends ever bother that woman again, I won't be so forgiving."

"I found it." Jenny entered the room, carrying a length of white nylon cord and a sharp knife.

"Good." Dan smiled at her. "Why don't you hold that gun on the fat guy, while I tie our foreign visitor up?"

She bent down, picking up the gun. Dan tried not to notice that she held it with an unnerving familiarity. Jenny sighed as she caught his grim expression.

"Dan, I grew up on an Oregon ranch," she reminded him. "My dad taught me to shoot before I was seven."

"Oh." A wave of relief washed over him.

Jenny shook her head. "Your imagination is not to be believed, McGee," she muttered. She reached down, feeling the prone man's pulse. "He's going to be all right."

"Too bad," Dan muttered, finishing up the task. Squatting down, he rolled Werner over, twisting the cord around the man's wrists, then looping it about his ankles, holding him totally harmless when he finally did come to.

He was just about ready to congratulate himself when the front door squeaked again. "Terrific," Dan muttered under his breath. "Do you think you could shoot that thing?"

"If I had to. To protect you," she whispered in a shaky little voice.

Dan wondered how he'd ever gotten so lucky and only hoped they were going to get out of here alive so he could spend the rest of his life telling Jenny how much he loved her.

Suddenly they were face to face with a pair of three-fifty-seven magnum revolvers.

"Nice of you to drop in," Dan said, lowering his weapon. Jenny followed suit, and was immediately wrapped in the circle of his arms.

"We came as soon as we got your message," Mike

Flaherty said, putting away his own gun. "We were going to tell you that we'd tracked down your assailants, but it looks like you've got everything under control."

"You FBI guys need to take a few pointers from CIA," Dan laughed, marveling at how brave Jenny had been when she'd chosen to stay and fight, rather than leaving him to the mercy of both men. Brave and crazy. And he loved her for both traits.

"Rick said she was a winner," Brian Schneider agreed. "He's going to miss her."

"She's not quitting," Dan stated calmly, knowing it was what he wanted even as he watched the look of shock come across Jenny's face.

"Dan—"

"Later," he advised her firmly.

It didn't take long for the agents to get the two men into their car, and from the way the Welshman was talking, Dan knew they'd latched onto an extremely cooperative witness. Every once in a while you get lucky, he thought with satisfaction.

"Dan?" Jenny asked softly, once they were seated on the floor in the middle of absolute chaos while she washed the dried blood from his face.

"Yeah, honey?"

"What did you mean about me not quitting?"

"Do you really want to?"

Her touch was tender as she soothed his newly split lip with the edge of the damp washcloth. "I'd do anything for you," she said, her voice trembling just a little.

"You've already proven that." He flinched as she touched a sensitive spot.

"I'm sorry," she murmured, touching her fingers to her lips, then pressing them lightly against his skin. "Does that mean you've changed your mind about us?"

Her voice cracked and she suddenly turned her head away, staring at the floor.

"What?" He reached out, cupping her chin with his fingers to bring her gaze back to him. Her dark eyes were bright with unshed tears. "Where the hell did you get that goofy idea?"

"I know how you feel about my work. So, if you don't care anymore, then . . ." She shrugged sadly as her voice drifted off.

"I thought the CIA only hired smart people. How did you slip by their screening process?"

"What do you mean by that?"

He had hoped for a flare of pride, but all he got was tears. He sighed, brushing the diamondlike moisture from her skin.

"I've watched my mother working for one cause or another my entire life," he explained. "The same with my dad, when he was alive. I'd never honestly try to stop you from doing what you believed in, Jenny."

He smiled down at her, brushing a light kiss against her trembling lips. "Besides, I wouldn't want to take the chance that you'd become bored with me and take off to seek some more exciting guy."

"Never," she breathed. "But if you don't like it, Dan, I'll quit."

"I'll probably always worry about you," he admitted honestly. "But I'm not Jimmy Morgan or your father, sweetheart. I don't want to keep you locked up . . . Besides, didn't you say it's only a part-time thing?"

"That's right."

"And you'll still have time for your husband?"

She nodded. "All the time he'd ever want."

"And our kids? Tracy and Travis?"

"Absolutely." Her eyes sparkled with new tears, but Dan

knew they were tears of joy. As he drew her into his arms, resting his chin on the top of her head, Dan's own eyes were suspiciously moist.

"You were right about this being a Pulitzer story," he murmured into her silken hair. "Too bad I can't write it."

She pulled her head back, her gaze curious. "Why not?"

"I wouldn't want to blow your cover."

"Oh. I hadn't thought of that."

"There's still a few of us journalists around with scruples, sweetheart."

They fell silent.

"Dan?"

"Yeah, honey?"

"Don't they give a Pulitzer for fiction, too?"

The idea took form, and the more he thought about the possibility, the more Dan liked it. There was just one thing. . . .

"Come on," he said suddenly, pulling her to her feet.

"Where are we going?"

"Back to the Fairmont Hotel," he replied with a charmingly boyish grin that was going to be reserved solely for Jenny Winslow McGee from now on. "I want to work on the final chapter."

"Final chapter?"

"Don't you believe in happy endings?"

"McGee," she answered, laughter in her voice, "you've been spying on me again. Happy endings are my second favorite secret passion."

"What's your first?"

Jenny's mouth touched Dan's and her arms curled around his neck. "Happy beginnings."

Look for these exciting contemporary romances soon, from Signet!

THROWN FOR A LOSS: LINC'S STORY by Sherryl Woods.
Attorney Linc Taylor was used to having women in his arms, but *Judge* Christina Davis? Both knew a relationship could ruin their careers . . . but when passion drove them to break their profession's unwritten law, Linc wondered what the final verdict would be—which one of them would be willing to choose between ambition and love. . . ?

PROMISES TO KEEP by JoAnn Robb. California Senator Eve Steele knew the issues—but lost all sense of diplomacy when it came to handling her estranged husband, Alex. Now Alex was running his own campaign—to win Eve back. His smoldering love made her forget everything, except that he still wanted a houseful of children and she wanted an office in the capitol! How *would* Eve handle her toughest opponent. . . ?

WILD IRISH ROSE by Joan Wolf. New York socialite Sara Underwood was instantly attracted to Irishman Daniel Riordan, who worked for Sara's wealthy grandfather. But Daniel was far too proud to be called a fortune-hunter and he did his best to avoid Sara. Could she soften his Irish stubborn streak with her love? Or would she never convince him he was all the fortune she'd ever want. . . ?

OF EARTH AND HIGH HEAVEN by Melinda McKenzie. Dr. Brooke Bryant had her feet on the ground but wanted to test her daring theories miles above it on a NASA space station. But first she had to get past top astronaut Harry Pritchard—and when she found herself in an intense affair with him, she had to decide if an earthbound existence was worth the price of her heavenly passion. . . .

Passionate Historical Romances from SIGNET

THE KISS FLOWER
by Gimone Hall

This month's sweeping new historical romance from Signet!

PETAL SOFT CARESSES
No man had ever kissed Susannah this way before. the Marquis de Silva towered over her, his manly strength making her feel helpless as a magnolia petal caught in the swirling waters of the Mississippi. And as this irresistibly handsome man pressed his lips to her willing mouth, the rush of hot desire was so sure and swift that Susannah forgot she was promised to another. . . .

BLOSSOMS OF SCARLET DESIRE
Susannah shivered in his embrace. Fate had brought this royal rogue into her life, and now a passion she could no longer deny threatened to carry her away from her beloved South. She feared this seductive stranger, yet craved his burning touch. And his masculine power reached out to claim her, she was ready to surrender herself to wild raging ecstasy. . . .

THE KISS FLOWER

☐ 0451-13846-5 $3.95, U.S./$4.50, Canada

Sweeping Sagas from SIGNET

Romantic Fiction from SIGNET

Romantic Reading from SIGNET

*Prices slightly higher in Canada

**Buy them at your local
bookstore or use coupon
on next page for ordering.**

Passionate Historical Romances from SIGNET

**Buy them at your local
bookstore or use coupon
on next page for ordering.**

SIGNET Regency Romances You'll Enjoy

(0451)

☐ **FALSE COLOURS** by Georgette Heyer. (131975—$2.50)†
☐ **AN INFAMOUS ARMY** by Georgette Heyer. (131630—$2.95)†
☐ **PISTOLS FOR TWO** by Georgette Heyer. (132483—$2.50)†
☐ **THE SPANISH BRIDE** by Georgette Heyer. (132769—$2.95)*
☐ **ROYAL ESCAPE** by Georgette Heyer. (133323—$2.95)†
☐ **POOR RELATION** by Marion Chesney. (128184—$2.25)*
☐ **THE VISCOUNT'S REVENGE** by Marion Chesney. (125630—$2.25)*
☐ **THE MARRIAGE MART** by Norma Lee Clark. (128168—$2.25)*
☐ **THE PERFECT MATCH** by Norma Lee Clark. (124839—$2.25)*
☐ **THE IMPULSIVE MISS PYMBROKE** by Norma Lee Clark. (132734—$2.50)*
☐ **A MIND OF HER OWN** by Anne MacNeill. (124820—$2.25)*
☐ **THE LUCKLESS ELOPEMENT** by Dorothy Mack. (129695—$2.25)*
☐ **THE BLACKMAILED BRIDEGROOM** by Dorothy Mack. (127684—$2.25)*
☐ **THE RELUCTANT ABIGAIL** by Miranda Cameron. (131622—$2.50)*
☐ **THE MEDDLESOME HEIRESS** by Miranda Cameron. (126165—$2.25)*
☐ **A SCANDALOUS BARGAIN** by Miranda Cameron. (124499—$2.25)*
☐ **THE FORTUNE HUNTER** by Elizabeth Hewitt. (125614—$2.25)*
☐ **A SPORTING PROPOSITION** by Elizabeth Hewitt. (123840—$2.25)*
☐ **CAPTAIN BLACK** by Elizabeth Hewitt. (131967—$2.50)*
☐ **BORROWED PLUMES** by Roseleen Milne. (098114—$1.75)†

*Prices slightly higher in Canada
†Not available in Canada
